Little Women Next Door

Sheila Solomon Klass

Holiday House / New York

For Anatol Elvis Klass—
who loved books even before
he could read.
S. S. K.

Letter on page 120 excerpted from *Transcendental Wild Oats*, by Louisa May Alcott, copyright © 1981, with permission from Harvard Common Press, 535 Albany Street, Boston, MA 02118, 888-657-3755. www.harvardcommonpress.com

Library of Congress Cataloging-in-Publication Data

Klass, Sheila Solomon.
Little women next door / Sheila Solomon Klass.—1st ed.
p. cm.
Summary: Recounts the efforts of Louisa May Alcott's family to establish
a utopian community known as Fruitlands in Massachusetts in 1843, as seen
through the eyes of the shy eleven-year-old girl next door.
ISBN 0-8234-1472-8 (hardcover)
1. Alcott, Louisa May, 1832–1888—Family—Juvenile fiction. [1. Alcott, Louisa May,
1832–1888—Family—Fiction. 2. Family life—Massachusetts. 3. Massachusetts—Fiction.]
I. Title.

PZ7.K67814 Li 2000
[Fic]—dc21   00-035016

Contents

1. The Strangers Who Wouldn't Eat Cheese

Newcomers.

I was admiring a spiderweb on my bedroom window during an afternoon rain shower when I caught sight of them. My heart began to drum so loud, I felt the thumps in my ears. It was the first of June, but gray and chilly and till that moment just an ordinary day.

Their old wagon was so loaded down, I expected it would sink in the mud. If it did, Pa would have to run out to help them. They'd come into our kitchen to dry off by the fire. And I might get to fix some chamomile tea for them.

"One driver . . . ," I counted. "Two girls . . . a woman with a small child . . . a boy holdin' on to what looks like a big statue . . . one more girl carrying a bundle like a baby wrapped in India rubber, and . . . three more men besides her. One of those men has a great beard!"

Slipping to the other side of the window as they passed, I strained to see more, sensing that these folks were different. Pa wouldn't like that one bit. He hated change. Pa believed in sameness.

Did different have to mean bad? Couldn't it mean just not the same? Couldn't it even mean better? Thinking that way was disobedient. Aunt Nell sometimes disagreed with Pa, but she was grown. I never wanted him to get all red-faced and angry at me.

Luckily, he wasn't in from milking yet.

If I hurried, I could give Aunt Nell the news. Though set in her ways and usually silent, when there were folks around she could turn sociable. A tall, thin farm woman, she wore her gray hair pinned up in tight braids round her head and spent her days doing chores: washing, cooking, cleaning, gardening, and sewing.

Daily she dressed the same, in a spotless gingham dress covered by a long white apron. That apron got put on at sunrise and taken off when she went to sleep. Except on Sundays, of course, when she dressed up fine for church. Or on the days when her rheumatism kept her to her bed in her flannel nightgown. Her rheumatism was fierce.

"Aunt Nell," I called as I came flying down the stairs. "N-N-New n-neighbors!"

"Mercy, Susan, calm yourself," she advised, and then she listened to my news attentively. When I was done, she checked to be sure she'd heard me right. "A beard?"

I nodded.

"And a statue? You sure, child?"

I nodded again.

"Well. That *is* something. Wait till Henry hears."

My news had discombobulated her, so the instant Pa walked into the kitchen, she began chattering about the strangers. He looked astonished. Aunt Nell was not a chatterer. Pa never did say too much either, but he had more opinions than she did. He felt real strong against whiskey drinking and slavery and swearing and idleness.

Pa was an *against* person.

Mostly, he just worked and worked. On Saturday night, bath night, he shaved extra close, sometimes nicking his face with that sharp straight razor. And each Sunday he put on a collar and a tie and the black suit that he'd been married in.

Pa looked much like Aunt Nell, who was his older sister, only he was taller and skinnier and mostly bald with thick gray eyebrows, and he wore spectacles. Now he was hearing her out careful. His eyebrows jumped like two loose caterpillars when she mentioned the statue and the beard.

After she was done talking, he thought awhile. "Must be odd folk," he said. He went on slowly as he worked things out in his head. "Who else'd buy that

Wyman farm with its poor land and scrubby orchard? Why, there ain't more than about ten old apple trees left standing."

He set to soaping himself, hands and arms up to the elbows, then rinsing off in the tin tub, brooding on what troubled him most. "A beard," he muttered as he dried himself. "Hard to believe."

In the year 1843, most Massachusetts men were clean-shaven, so Pa couldn't allow there was a beard on a new neighbor.

"I'm going to be neighborly," Aunt Nell said briskly, taking the towel when he was done. "When folks just move in they got a sight of heavy work to do. I'm fixing to take them some of my fresh cheese and apple butter." She looked to me. "Susan, you hang this towel in the pantry."

I did as I was told. In the pantry, I buried my face in the towels on the rack because I was grinning like a fool. Aunt Nell was going to make friends with the newcomers. I moved quietly to the doorway and listened in.

"You sure you want to walk out so far?" Pa asked.

"My legs are fine today. Rheumatism's sleeping for a change. Yes, I want to go."

Ordinarily Pa wouldn't have objected. He believed in being a good neighbor, but the mention of the beard must have put him off. "Best mind your own affairs," he advised.

"It's the Christian thing to do, Henry." Aunt Nell knew how to get around Pa, him being a churchman and a deacon.

He sighed.

Slipping out of her apron, she got her bonnet off the peg and tied it under her chin. Then she came into the pantry to get the cheese and wrap it in a fresh white cloth. While doing that, she asked me, "Please, Susan, fetch me a quart jar of apple butter."

I did, and then as I stood there holding it she looked long at me, and an idea seemed to come to her. "Would you like to come along?"

She took me by surprise. Though I was itching with curiosity about the newcomers—especially about the girls—she knew I didn't like to go anywhere where I had to meet people.

Whenever my chores were done, I spent most of my time alone, roaming the fields, spotting birds and butterflies, catching bugs to play with, and visiting with small animals. I'd sit so still they'd trust me and come close and let me pet them. Sometimes I made the raccoons and squirrels my schoolmates and asked them to spell words or do sums. Of course, they never answered, so I was always smartest. This was my favorite game; I longed to go to school.

I also liked to pick daisies and knot their stems to make long flower-chain necklaces for our cows. The cows looked beautiful, but they didn't appreciate their jewelry. Mostly they ate their necklaces right away.

I played tunes on grass whistles, and I collected pretty wildflowers. The brightest were my favorites: purple jacks-in-the-pulpit and scarlet Indian paintbrushes and yellow buttercups and black-eyed Susans. I brought them home to sit in the milk-glass pitcher on our table.

I could talk easy enough to a woodchuck or a field mouse. But I stammered whenever I spoke to real people.

Aunt Nell was gentle with me. That was her way.

"I would like it if you came along, Susan. I'm always glad of your company."

I was already shaking my head no, even though my heart was crying yes. I wanted to go. But meeting new folks scared me.

"I could use your help," Aunt continued, "because I'm not so surefooted anymore. I can carry the cheese, but I don't guess I'd better tote the apple butter in a glass jar."

Those girls and the boy, too, had to taste Aunt's delicious conserves. They turned a plain piece of bread into an apple tart.

"I'll go," I made myself answer quick, "if Pa allows."

She was pleased. "I'll see to your pa. Get your bonnet. And take a shawl against the dew."

She fretted because I was often ailing with sniffles and rashes and fever or whatever ague there was around. This past spring had been the worst, with me spending more than three weeks in bed.

Aunt Nell nursed me, feeding me broth and rose hip tea and milk toast. I heard her complaining to Pa one time that I was like flypaper. "That Susan catches everything that's floating around and then it sticks to her tight," she grumbled.

Since getting out of bed, I'd been poorly, hardly moving outdoors. So I took down my plaid shawl as my aunt went inside and spoke softly to Pa.

I heard his surprise. "What?" he said. "She wants to go along and meet the odd neighbors?"

She answered him, again softly, but I picked out the words *glass jar* and *rheumatism*. Then he said I might go.

Clutching the jar tightly, I minded each step I took. I, Susan Wilson, then past ten years old, had never been face-to-face with a man with a real beard. Oh, I'd seen some from afar and pictures in a book. And right before Pa shaved each week, he had brown fuzz on his upper lip and chin and cheeks, but that wasn't a true mustache or beard. So I was mighty interested.

My pa farmed the family land near Harvard village about a dozen miles northwest of Concord. In 1775 the American militia had fired the first shots against the British right there, starting the whole Revolution.

7

Since those important gunshots, it seemed to me, not much had happened in our countryside. Except last April on a nearby farm, a cow had a two-headed calf. Pa didn't think to take me to see it, but he saw it and told about it.

Mostly we did chores, went to church, and lived quiet.

In the general store or at church each Sunday, I kept on seeing the same folks, our neighbors: the young like me and the grown-ups, and there were no beards.

Together, my aunt and I went down the path and across the great meadow, me carrying the apple butter while she held the cheese flat across her hands. Twice we rested on the stone fence, sitting while Aunt favored her legs for a few minutes.

I could hardly wait. Three big-girl neighbors and a young one to play with—and a boy—and, besides them, a beard and a statue.

When we got to the red-painted, two-story farmhouse on the next property, there was a new wooden sign swinging on a pole over the front door. Each letter was shaped of twigs then nailed neatly to a board.

"*Fruitlands*," I read aloud.

"Fancy that," Aunt Nell said. "They only just come, and afore they even unpacked their pots and skillets, they hung up a sign."

A girl about my age opened the door at my aunt's knock.

"Greetings," the girl said. "Welcome to Fruitlands." Then daintily lifting the hem of her frock at either side, she curtseyed real low. She was way taller than me and almost as thin, and she had lovely gray eyes and thick brown hair in two tight plaits to her waist.

"Fruitlands?" Aunt Nell said, taken aback. "Since when?"

"Since this afternoon." The girl smiled at us. "Isn't it a lovely name?"

Aunt nodded. I did, too.

"Because we are going to live on the fruit of the land."

Ten scrubby old apple trees, Pa had said. How would they ever live on that?

Aunt Nell spoke up. "We're your neighbors over on the next farm. Susan here saw your wagon go by. I thought it being moving day, you might be able to use some apple butter and fresh cheese for your dinner."

"That is most kind, ma'am. Actually, my sisters and I adore cheese." She looked a bit sad for a second. "But since we are Consociates now, we are not allowed to eat it."

"Consociates?" Aunt asked.

"One big family living here all together and sharing everything equally—"

"Ask the visitors in, Louisa," a woman's voice called from inside.

"Yes, Marmee," she called back. Then to us she said, "Please come in."

9

Just then the mother came toward us herself, leading a grinning small girl with a loose sunburst of hair, the yellowest I'd ever seen.

"Good evening," she said in a soft voice.

She was a tall, plump lady in a loose, shapeless dress; she had flashing dark eyes and chestnut hair done up tight in a bun. "I am Abigail May Alcott. Here, I'm called Sister Abigail. You have met my daughter, Louisa May. And this little one is baby May. Would you like to sit down for a bit?"

"Oh no, no thank you. I'm Nell Wilson. I keep house for my widowed brother and this young'un of his, Susan, on the next farm." Aunt Nell's words rushed out in a stream. "We know you just moved in. We figured we'd walk over with some vittles for your supper." She didn't know whether to offer the cheese, but I held out the jar of apple butter.

Sister Abigail asked Louisa to set the jar on the table. Then she smiled at me and said, "How very thoughtful. Thank you so much, Susan." To my aunt she said, "I shall not take the cheese, for it would go to waste. We do not eat cheese here."

"So your daughter said. No cheese ever?" Aunt Nell showed her amazement.

"No food that comes from any animals. We're vegetarians."

"No milk either?"

Sister Abigail shook her head.

"No butter? No eggs?" Aunt Nell was having trouble believing her ears. "Heavens, what do you cook for dinner?"

Sister Abigail laughed. "There's always purslane and dandelions growing wild for salad. And potatoes. But do come inside for a few minutes and sit, and perhaps I can explain."

Aunt Nell hesitated, while I stood there praying she'd accept.

"Marmee," Louisa said, "perhaps Susan would like to see my favorite doll while you and her aunt chat." She turned to me. "I walked all the way here carrying the doll to keep it safe. That is why she's already unpacked."

"Wrapped in I-I-India rubber?" I said, pointing my finger at her excitedly. "I saw f-from my window."

She was delighted. "Did you wonder about my precious bundle? I hope you thought it was jewels and mysterious treasure. Gold ducats buried by pirates—"

I never thought of it!

Aunt Nell said, "We'll stay a little while."

"Come this way." Sister Abigail led her into the house. "The men are setting up the furniture upstairs, but we've several chairs down here." She began to explain as they went. "I'm sure our sign surprised you. Brother Everett came on ahead to make it. Let me explain about Fruitlands . . ."

And then just one second later—too late for Aunt to see—it happened.

First we heard loud footsteps, and then two great tall men came traipsing through carrying a stack of long boards, one man holding each end.

"Shelves," Louisa explained, "for our books."

They went right by with the boards into a side room, me staring after them, because there was one thing she hadn't mentioned.

The beard!

The man in front had a thick white fur piece on his chin. It was shaped like a spade and hung clear down his chest almost to his waist.

I saw it for myself and it was wonderful.

I was too shy to stare at it real hard, but I did take one long direct look just short of a stare. Then I ducked my head.

Afterward I was sorry. I figured that I might have looked longer, because a man who grows a beard must want you to look at it. Anyway, I was proud I saw it.

It beat any two-headed calf.

2. I Learn Some Magic Charms

"Come."

I stood fast till Louisa took my hand and together we went into the large kitchen. It was shabby, with a crooked floor and a sooty old fireplace that didn't look as if it'd ever been cleaned. It wasn't near as nice as Aunt's kitchen. All around was mess and clutter, piles of pots and utensils and baskets mixed up with sacks and boxes.

"It must be h-h-hard to move," I said. "I've always l-l-lived on our farm. I can't imagine l-living elsewhere."

"Oh, we move almost every year. It's an adventure. I love adventures," Louisa said. "I write them down in my diary."

"What's a diary?"

She seemed surprised. "It's a notebook where you write down what happens most days."

"But most d-d-days are the s-s-same."

"Oh no!" She shook her head. "Different things happen all the time. You must have a diary, Susan."

I shook my head. "I w-wouldn't know what to write in it."

"You can write poems in it, and stories and plays."

"I'd l-l-like that. Excuse my st-stammer." I could feel myself blushing. This was the longest conversation I'd ever had with a complete stranger.

"My father is a schoolmaster. Last year he had a pupil named Tad who stammered almost every word," Louisa said. "If you take your time, speak slowly, and don't worry about it, it will vanish." She said it surely, as if she were making a promise. "In fact, you can chase it away."

I shook my head. I'd tried. I knew I couldn't do that.

"Watch!" Louisa ordered. "Imagine you're King Alfonso of Spain. A very powerful king." Stretching her forefinger over her upper lip as a mustache, she scowled fiercely. "Begone, vile stammer!" she exclaimed. "Do not darken my palace door!" Then she stamped her foot so hard the piled pots rattled. "Now you try it."

"Uh-uh."

She looked disappointed. "Oh, Susan. Don't you want to chase the trouble away?"

I did want to, with all my heart.

"Then say it!"

So I screwed up my face, scowled, made the finger-mustache, and repeated the magic words. Then I stamped my foot so hard the kettle on top of the pot pile fell off.

Quickly, I set the kettle back in place.

"Bravo!" Louisa cheered.

My heart beat as if I'd been running. "Was there r-really a K-King Alfonso of Spain?"

She shrugged. "What does it matter? Just repeat the charm whenever the stammer traps you. You'll be in command of yourself. Father says that is the key to building character."

In command of myself? I always did as I was told, and I most always did what I was expected to do. That's how I was raised. How could I tell her that I never once in my whole life felt in command of myself?

"I c-c-could never say that out loud in front of others, Louisa. I just c-couldn't. They'd think me odd."

"Well, you can say it here at Fruitlands. No one will think anything of it," she said. "And I guess you can just think it to yourself inside your head. Like a wish. But it works better out loud with the mustache."

Now she was grinning at me. "You'll see. It's magic. And I know one other spell you can try. This one is from Shakespeare, and you won't need a mustache because it's *Lady* Macbeth." Louisa straightened up. "You curl up your tongue inside for a second," she said, then she spoke the charm: "Out, damned stutter! Out, I say!"

I was shocked. "Did Sh-Shakespeare use that word?"

"What word?"

I whispered it. "*Damned*."

"Sure, it's a perfectly good word. It's in the Bible. Try these magic charms, Susan. My father's pupil, Tad, spoke much better after a while. Only when he was overexcited—like on his birthday when he got into his bed and my pet frog, Hercules, was under his quilt as a present—then he stammered a bit." She giggled. "He jumped, too, higher than Hercules."

Under the table, safe from the confusion of the move, was the loveliest doll with a rosy-cheeked china face and dark curls, on top of which sat a gold paper crown. "I'm too old to play with her, but I love her best," Louisa said after we'd crawled under there.

We sat there awhile, me holding the doll while she explained that every day the doll got a new name. "Today she is Queen Penelope of Ithaca in ancient Greece, who waited twenty years for her husband, Odysseus, to sail back from the Trojan War."

"Why'd it take him so long?"

"His ship got lost. Other men, back in Greece, kept saying he was dead, and they wanted to marry Penelope. She didn't want to marry anyone else, so she started a weaving and told men that when the weaving was finished, she would remarry.

"All day she wove, then late every night she sneaked down the stairs, barefooted and very quiet, and she unraveled it so that it never got finished till her husband returned."

"Didn't anybody c-catch on?"

Louisa shook her head. "No. Though the Greek men were very smart, Penelope was smarter." She shrugged. "Tomorrow my doll will be Cleopatra, queen of Egypt, who was so sad she killed herself by letting an asp—that's a kind of snake—bite her."

I shivered because I was deathly afraid of snakes, but I wanted to hear more. Louisa knew wonderful stories.

Just then I heard Aunt Nell calling me and I had to scramble out from under the table. And while I was brushing myself off and looking around, sure enough my eyes lit on the statue. It was just the shoulders and the head of some old man—who also had a beard.

"Who's that? Your gr-grandpa?"

"Oh, no!" She laughed merrily. "That's Socrates."

"Wh-Wh-Wh . . . ?" My mouth blew air and refused to make the sound. I was about to give up when I saw Louisa's hand out and her fingers coaxing the words from me.

Quickly, I curled my tongue, then spoke very boldly, "*Out, damned stutter! Out, I say!* Who was Socrates?"

"He was a great teacher in Greece more than two thousand years ago."

"Queen Penelope's country?"

She nodded.

"Why's he h-h-here in your house, Louisa?"

"Because my father admires him."

"Oh," I said, as if I understood. I didn't.

"Susan," she said softly, "would you call me Louey instead of Louisa? I like it better now that I'm going to be eleven."

I nodded, pleased, and told her I, too, was looking forward to my eleventh birthday.

"I knew it!" Her eyes sparkled. "You and I can be best friends! Would you like a nickname?"

"No." I answered sharply. Then I saw she was disappointed, so I added, "I like my name a lot."

My aunt called a second time. "Susan, we must get back to fix supper."

It was hard to leave. We had so much to tell each other. "Coming," I called, amazed that I didn't need King Alfonso or Lady Macbeth. "Coming, Aunt."

Louisa clapped her hands with pleasure. Then she explained hurriedly, "I have the nicest sisters in the world, but I have been dreaming of being best friends with someone. Like Damon and Pythias. Or Jonathan and David." She scowled. "Those old stories never tell about girls being best friends. But you are perfect," she said, "exactly my own age." Then she stopped and looked at me hard. "Can you keep secrets?"

I nodded. Yes. *Yes*.

"Wonderful. That is . . . unless you already have a best friend?"

"No friends, except birds and raccoons and bugs. And no sisters either."

"Do you like to be in plays?" she asked.

"I d-don't know. I n-n-never was."

"Oh!"—she clapped her hands—"You'll love it. You can be a duke or a princess. Anything your heart desires."

"C-could I be Lady Macbeth?" I didn't know who she was, but I already knew her speech.

"Of course."

"But . . . I might st-stammer."

"I could write parts for a character who stammers. Until you conquer it."

"Out, damned stutter! Out, I say!" I tried it again just for the fun of it. Saying *damned* felt so wicked.

Aunt Nell was at the door waiting. Wishing them well in the new house, she reached for my hand.

A door closed overhead. "Ah, Miss Wilson—stay a moment more," Sister Abigail urged. "I think my husband's coming. Please wait and meet him."

At the head of the stairs stood a tall, slender man in a black suit covered with dust. "Callers?" he said. "How nice."

Our hostess chuckled. "This is my husband disguised as a dustman."

"I have just cleaned out the dirtiest room in the world." He brushed at his sleeves. "But do not think that because I am begrimed, my vision is dimmed. It is clearer than ever."

"These folks live on the next farm," his wife explained. "They've brought us a gift of apple butter."

"What a good omen! How generous of you!" He began to hurry down the stairs. "Welcome to Fruitlands, wel—"

In his hurry, he misstepped and tripped on a stair. His wife reached out and grabbed his dusty elbow, propping him up. She saved him just in time.

He smiled at her gratefully as she helped him straighten up. "Thank you, my dear Abigail."

Then he turned to us, and, still smiling, he said, "Welcome to our New Eden!" And covered though he was with dust, he then bowed low from the waist.

This is certainly the bowingest family, I thought.

Face-to-face, he was a kind looking man with bright blue eyes and a dimple in his chin. His hair came almost to his shoulders. He stood very straight. Truly, his clothes looked as if he had used himself to sweep the dirty floor.

After more "excuse me"s for his appearance, he introduced himself. "Bronson Alcott—Brother Bronson."

His wife spoke our names, and he said he was very glad to meet us. Oddly, instead of just addressing himself to my aunt and paying me no mind—the way grown-up folks usually did—he turned first to me and gave me his particular attention.

"You are called Susan? So is the yellow daisy—genus *Rudbeckia*—one of my favorite wildflowers."

"She is named for that flower," Aunt explained. "Her mother, who has passed on, had the same name and chose it for her."

"Ah," he said softly. "Do you go to school, child?"

I shook my head.

"Speak up."

"Susan stammers badly, so she is shy," Aunt Nell said. "We do sums and reading and writing at home when we can. She can read well but not out loud because of the stammer."

"Miss Wilson, it would be better for Susan if you let her speak for herself," he suggested mildly.

Telling Aunt Nell that was about as useful as telling a mother robin, "Shove your baby bird out of the nest and let her get her own worms." Aunt Nell would never do it. She preferred to speak for me. And I much preferred for her to do it. She always protected me.

Now she smoothed my hair. "Susan doesn't talk much but she's smart. She is acquainted with every bug and

21

every flower in the countryside. And in arithmetic—why, I get her to check my butter and cheese accounts regular, and just yesterday she caught two errors. Trouble is, she's not strong. She was ailing all this spring."

"She does look a little peaked," he agreed, "but the summer sun will soon restore her."

Louisa broke in. "Susan does not have a diary, Father. May we give her one?"

"If her aunt does not object. Miss Wilson, may we present Susan with a little notebook so that she can keep a private record of her ideas?"

Aunt Nell had to mull that over.

She was plainly of two minds. She knew Pa would say right off that a diary was outright foolishness. But seeing me standing there on tippytoes, bursting with wanting it so bad, I guess she figured it would do no harm. Even if Pa did grumble. "That's very kind of you," she consented.

Louisa immediately scrambled off to dig among the boxes, and she soon found and handed over to her father a thin blue paper-covered notebook, which he passed on to me. "Here, Susan. This is for you," he said.

"Th-Thank you. But wh-wh-what do I write in it?"

"Your thoughts," he said. "Your dreams and your ideas."

To my aunt he explained, "It encourages the habit of reflection." His blue eyes gleamed at me.

"I am a schoolmaster, Miss Wilson, and I will be giving the children lessons here. I would be glad to include Susan if you like. I can help her with the stammer. Next week when we are thoroughly set up, if she would like to come in the early mornings . . . "

My aunt bit her lower lip.

"Oh, yes, pl-please, Aunt, m-may I?" I begged.

"We really haven't means to pay for schooling . . . ," she began.

"I wouldn't dream of charging for lessons," he said.

"But—" Aunt Nell seemed confused.

"That's what Fruitlands is all about. This is an experiment in escaping from money worries—from commercialism. My friend Charles Lane and I have plans to build a paradise here: cottages, fountains, orchards . . . ." As he spoke, his eyes were no longer on us but looking way off in the distance.

His wife smiled. "My husband has a glorious vision."

"You both are very kind," Aunt Nell said. "I'll have to ask her pa."

"Tell him she'll learn here, and she'll run about in the sunshine. I believe in lots of play outdoors and exercise for children."

"Best of all," his wife added, "the girls would love for her to come. What could be better medicine than friends for a child?"

"I'm pleased to have met you," Aunt said. "I don't go about visiting, because of my rheumatism, but I wanted to make you welcome."

"We appreciate that more than you know," Sister Abigail said, and she took Aunt's hands and enfolded them in hers for a moment.

As we started down the outside steps, Aunt Nell began to mumble to herself, "What could be better medicine than friends for a child? I ask you that, Henry." She was rehearsing what she would say to Pa.

I knew the answer to that question.

Nothing. Nothing could be better than friends.

I had dreamed so long of going to school, of learning and playing with other children. Idle dreams. Aunt Nell was my teacher and the kitchen table my desk. Aunt Nell was kind and smart. What right had I to complain? Absolutely no right.

So, of course, I kept my mouth shut tight. Because I knew the rules. Only grown-ups were entitled to opinions. Only men, really. I was a child. And a girl. Nothing was ever up to me—not what I wore, not what I ate, not what I did.

Children were to be seen but not heard.

3. God's Handmaiden Gets Butterfingers

Running to catch up with Aunt, I marveled at how quick her feet forgot about their rheumatism. As we made our way back home, those feet moved so fast that I had to skip to keep up. Enough new neighbors might cure Aunt Nell's rheumatism entirely.

In her hands she still carried the cheese.

Soon's we got through the front door, Pa asked her, "Did ya see the beard?"

"No," she said. "The men were working upstairs."

I saw it, I could've told him. But he never asked me.

And, to be truthful, I couldn't have told him even if he'd asked, because whenever I tried to talk to Pa I stammered something terrible. And he had no patience with it. It was as if he thought I was stubborn and doing it on purpose or it was a birth fault—some bad thing. It made him tetchy.

Mindful of supper, Aunt gave me carrots and potatoes to pare at the kitchen table while she and Pa talked. First she told him about all the Alcotts, then she went on, "There's an Englishman, Charles Lane, with his young son, William. This Charles Lane is a great thinker who crossed the ocean just to live here. Besides all of them, there are three other men. Eleven all together."

"Kin?" Pa guessed. "Whole family going to farm together?"

"Not exactly."

"What's that?"

"They aren't blood kin, though they call each other Brother and Sister. They have this idea that they want to live together in peace without any need for money—as one human family."

What a grand idea, I thought as I peeled potatoes. All those brothers and sisters and uncles and aunts in one house. It sounded perfect. No one could ever be lonely in such a family.

Pa peered at Aunt Nell over the top of his spectacles. "Who cooked up this crack-brained plan?"

"Brother Bronson and Charles Lane thought it up together, but Lane paid for the farm. They're sort of part-ners. The Englishman seems to do most of the thinking and planning."

"Well, it's his money bought the land...." Pa shrugged. "But he don't know beans about farming, that's for sure. It's worn-out land."

"Brother Bronson figured that, him being from farm folk. He warned that the land was no longer fertile, but Lane insisted because he fell in love with that old house on Prospect Hill—"

Pa coughed suddenlike till Aunt Nell smacked him on the back to help him stop.

"The view of the Nashua valley and Mount Wachusett a ways off grabbed him," Aunt Nell finished her news.

It took Pa a good while to digest all that information. "Nobody with a crumb of common sense buys a farm for the view."

"Beautiful surroundings are mighty important to these folks' souls." Aunt Nell paused and rested a bit, and when she talked again there was surprise in her tone. "I never thought about our countryside that way. I mean, it is very pretty and all, but—"

"Humph!" Pa's head began to say no afore she was done.

Why couldn't he credit what he was hearing? Our woods and mountains and meadows were beautiful. I ducked my head so he couldn't see I was having disobedient thoughts.

"Sister Abigail allowed they were a *Consociate* family— that means all partners. Come to establish a paradise."

"Humph. Why're you still holding the cheese? Your cheese not good enough for all them angels?"

I saw Aunt hesitate. "The funny thing is, they were mighty glad to have my apple butter—"

"Maybe they heard it was the best apple butter in the county." Pa took powerful pride in Aunt Nell's cooking and preserving. Her covered dishes were usually the first gobbled up at church suppers. And her fried fish—especially perch—won grand prize at the Harvard Village Fish Fry on May Day, last two years running.

She smiled. "It seems as if they don't eat cheese."

"They must be fools," Pa said. "Coming to farm and being so partickalar. Nothing like fresh cheese for breakfast."

"They don't eat anything that comes from animals. They aren't going to wear anything comes from animals either, or even any cotton cloth, 'cause they're against slavery."

"What? They going to go about uncovered?" Pa seemed scandalized at the idea.

"They'll all wear linen."

"They got to wear shoes, don't they?" Pa demanded.

"Now—but they're looking for a substitute. Maybe tree bark."

This was too much for Pa. It left him dumbfounded.

Tree bark. I would love a pair of tree-bark shoes. Maybe with vines for laces and tiny baby leaves at the end for tassels. Or flowers. Bluebells.

"They seem nice enough folks, Henry," Aunt Nell continued. "Kind and gentle. Just sort of foolish. Dreamers."

She paused and rubbed her hand back and forth over her mouth, getting ready for the big one.

I covered my eyes. My fingers were about as crossed as they could get.

She just spoke it straight out. "Bronson Alcott is a schoolmaster and will be glad if Susan comes mornings for lessons. Free!"

"She's not going anywhere without shoes," Pa answered fiercely.

"No, you don't understand. They don't force anyone to believe what they believe. Each person lives according to his conscience."

Aunt Nell stopped talking. She waited, but all she got in return was silence. After a long hesitation, she then took up the subject again. "The schoolmaster said he could help Susan with her stammer."

"I haven't cash to pay for schooling."

"They wouldn't charge. It'd be pleasure for the child, as well as a chance at learning. And an opportunity to work on speaking plain."

"I don't take charity. She can already read and write her ABC's good, and she's true with numbers. She can't talk, but I don't believe anyone can fix that."

He paused and then bobbed his head, agreeing with himself. "What does a girl need with more learning than that? It'll only clutter up her head. She needs to know how to sew and cook. Woman's work. You been too easy on her, Nell."

"She does her chores. You know she's not been well. She's had a hard childhood. I do what I can and I love her dearly, but I'm not proper company for a ten-year-old."

His head was saying no. Saying no came more natural to my pa than breathing. My hopes shriveled up like the carrot scrapings in the bucket. I hate you, Pa, I thought, and trembled at my own evil.

Aunt Nell didn't give up. "Learning never hurt a body. Susan needs other children. What could be better medicine for a child than friends?" Her voice trembled.

"Woman's work is what she needs more training in," Pa repeated. His fist thumped the table. "No. That's final."

Aunt Nell came and collected the vegetables and asked me to put the cheese in the springhouse where we kept foods cool. Very slowly and sadly, I started on my errand. And then I couldn't help myself: I began to bawl along the way.

A girl might not need to know more, but she might want to know more. She might want to know lots more about all the wonderful things and places and people in the world. She might even want to know everything. What was wrong with that?

Nothing! I wanted to shout it at Pa, but if I shouted only the cows and pigs would've heard. Probably I would have stammered.

What a terrible ending to an exciting day.

This day I had found then lost a best friend.

Louey knew all about Lady Macbeth and stammering and diaries and Socrates, about so many things. Before meeting her, I hadn't realized how lonely I was. And now I'd be even lonelier, knowing that just a little ways off from me was paradise. And I'd lost it.

Well, Aunt Nell set to cooking the evening meal. She was furious with Pa. I could feel it in the windup way she was acting, so sharp and distant as if her mind was out for a walk somewhere else and not in our kitchen. She handed me the tableware without saying a word. And when the food was ready, she went and rang the bell we used to call Pa in from the fields when he was sitting right there near her.

While Pa said grace, I said my own private prayer. First I thanked God for my food and for the new neighbors, then I asked Him for a favor, and when I looked to Aunt her eyes were shut and I knew what she was asking. We ate lima bean soup and cold chicken, mashed potatoes, and carrots. There was no talking at table. The only sounds were soup-slurping and chewing and the clatter of cutlery on the plates.

The conversation about the strangers had been exhausting, and, this night, my aunt was silent-angry; but generally my folks believed that talking was something you didn't do unless you had to. Since words came so hard to me, I was quietest of all. Especially at table.

Dessert was a surprise: baked rosy juicy apples, their centers stuffed with cores of raisins, and maple sugar melted all over them like soft candy. My favorite sweet in the whole world, but even that didn't cheer me up this night.

Aunt Nell finally spoke. "I have a second apple for you, Susan."

I shook my head.

"You all right, child?"

I never turned down seconds of baked apple.

I nodded.

I did the dishes afterward while Aunt Nell sewed near the lamp and Pa rocked. When she came into my bedroom to bid me goodnight, she bent down near my ear to say, "Don't fret. You might get to go to school."

"It would t-t-take a miracle," I said, and turned my face into my pillow.

"God works miracles," she whispered, then added mysteriously, "but even He sometimes needs a hand-maiden." She squeezed my shoulder. "Pray to Him."

I began immediately, mumbling over and over, "Please, Lord, let Pa change his mind." I kept count. Just past six hundred, I fell asleep.

By next morning, my aunt had turned into another person. She was no longer Nell Wilson. Overnight she had become Nell Butterfingers. Which was kind of a *hand*maiden, I guess.

Whenever Pa was in the house, puttering or rocking or reading his Bible, she began dropping things: first the ladle and then the rolling pin, then the skillet. Her racket with the kitchenwares signaled that she was hopping mad. Silence last night didn't work, so she was trying noise.

She added to the dropping ruckus by starting to sniffle—like she had a winter cold in June. Aunt Nell could have won first prize at the county fair; she was a prize-winning sniffler. And her anger floated around in the air so thick I could breathe it in.

So all day Saturday and all day Sunday, except for church, she went about dropping and sniffling, dropping and sniffling. It was something to hear. Especially after Friday night's graveyard quiet.

Sunday evening Aunt and I were cross-stitching a tablecloth just before my bedtime. The big scissors kept falling off Aunt's lap. Suddenly, Pa reared up out of his chair and turned to her. "All right, Nell. You win. Those new folks are bound to need produce from the garden. You think if I brought them a few basketfuls regular-like, that might do to pay for Susan's schooling?"

"Henry"—Aunt Nell clapped her hands together—"that's a wonderful idea."

My mind raced. I summoned up all the magic in my power. King Alfonso (without a mustache): Begone, vile stammer! Do not darken my palace door! I commanded silently. Quickly, I curled my tongue. Lady Macbeth: Out, damned stutter! Out, I say! Finally, with all the control I could command, I stood up and faced Pa, and I spoke slow and clear. "Thank you, Pa. Thank you so much."

He stared at me, and his eyebrows caterpillared up. Way up.

"I'll learn a lot. I promise."

I didn't stammer one word.

Not a single one.

Not one.

Dear Diary,

I have a friend at last. A best friend!

She and I will tell each other secrets that no one else knows.

Her name is Louisa May Alcott. But she'd rather be called just plain Louey. Her father is a dusty schoolmaster. He says he will try to help me speak normal.

He and Mr. Lane, his friend, are building a paradise next door called Fruitlands. Pa don't think much of their idea.

Everyone at Fruitlands will practice being good and kind till they are all perfect. I will watch carefully to learn how.

I am writing down my ideas and private thoughts. It's hard, but I hope I will get better at doing it.

Aunt Nell (God's handmaiden) dropped all the wares and made a racket till Pa changed his mind about schooling me at Fruitlands. Bless Aunt Nell. Bless Pa, too, I guess.

And especially bless Louey. And her doll, Queen Penelope, who became Queen Cleopatra, who killed herself with an asp (which is a snake). Bless Lady Macbeth and King Alfonso, who work charms and help me speak.

And make the Alcott children and even the boy, William, like me and want to be my friends!

How lucky I am to be living next door to paradise!

Amen.

4. Pa Comes Face-to-Face with the Beard

On Monday morning next, I rose early and went to work with soap and a facecloth, scrubbing my neck and my ears so that I'd be all clean and ready for my schooling. My ears got particular attention 'cause I wanted to be sure to hear every word spoken at Fruitlands. Words there could be magical.

I put on my church dress, white dimity with blue raised stripes and a lace collar. Aunt Nell had sewed it by my bedside when I was sick in the springtime. The dress was full-skirted and didn't show my skinniness so much.

It was fun to get all dressed up on a weekday. Aunt Nell came in from her rose garden to do my hair. "Your pa's going to walk over there with you," she told me. "He'll bring them some fresh corn and lettuce and beans and potatoes. He wants to know what kind of lessons Mr. Alcott gives."

I was joyful. Pa and I had never once gone walking. Aunt pieced two blue hair ribbons right in with my braids and tied them in big bows. "Blue shows fine in light brown hair," she said, passing me the hand mirror.

I looked at the small thin face with freckles sprinkled across the nose like maple sugar. I smiled. My face did look special that morning. Kind of pretty. My dark eyes were shiny as marbles. Maybe even as bright as my mother's eyes had been. "Do I look like my ma, Aunt?" I asked.

Ma's eyes had been the shiningest dark-near-to-black that Aunt Nell ever did see. Bright yet gentle as a doe's.

"More and more like her every day." Aunt Nell used a finger to brush a tear from her eye. She had loved my mother from the first moment she saw her.

Though I favored my ma, I wasn't at all like her. Much younger than Pa and Aunt, she'd been quick-tongued with a right easy laugh that made the old farmhouse lively. Maybe that was what kept Pa distant from me. Sometimes he'd look up at me suddenlike and be startled—like he was disappointed to find *me* there.

"Ready," Aunt Nell declared me set to go at last.

Pa and I started out, him carrying the basket filled with vegetables on his shoulder and going at a good speed. I walked a pace or two behind him, excited and scared.

As we neared the neighbors' house we heard the regular sound of an ax, and, sure enough, there was someone at the woodpile splitting logs in the cool of the morning.

The beard!

Oh no, I thought, trembling. Pa will have a turn-around fit. It's good-bye to schooling.

The woodchopper rested the ax head on the ground and leaned on the handle as we approached. "Morning," he said. "I'm Joseph Palmer—Brother Joseph."

"Henry Wilson," Pa told him. "Farm next to your'n."

"Good morning, young lady. I think I saw you in our kitchen on moving day."

"M-M-M-Morning," I said, nodding. I thought about a curtsey, but Pa would think I was daft. "I'm Susan."

"Come to learn? That's good. Brother Bronson has the teaching gift. He's taught school in Connecticut and Philadelphia and Boston. He's wonderful with children."

Pa just stood, listening.

"I saw wonder in your eyes the other day," Brother Joseph said to me. "I guess you never saw such a beard before?"

"N-n-never." I shook my head.

"Child, this beard is mighty costly." He stroked the edges of it fondly. "It cost me a whole year in jail."

Pa couldn't believe his ears. "How come?"

"I let this beard grow 'cause I like it. The good Lord gave it to me and it's mine. But you know how it is with some folks. They like to mind other folks' business. Tell 'em what to do?

"One evening I was walking down the street in Worcester, when along came these three ruffians. They took sight of me and they didn't fancy my beard. So they decided they would separate me from it and it from me."

"Oh n-n-no!" I gasped.

"That's just exactly what I told myself. *Oh no!* So when they jumped me, I pulled out my pocketknife and defended myself. One of them got hurt—just a scrape, I'm pleased to say."

He looked at us real serious. "I don't believe in doing bodily harm to another human. I was only trying to defend myself. Then I was arrested, and I went to jail. The judge said I had to pay a fine. I said, no sir, I wouldn't do it.

"Why should I, when I was simply protecting what was mine? I told that judge, 'The way I figure it, if God in His wisdom gave me the beard, who is mortal man to undo His work?'"

"Amen," Pa said, but he said it weak, not loud like he calls it out in church.

"I wouldn't pay one penny. They held me in jail a whole year and treated me just terrible, but I kept my beard. So I don't mind if folks stare at it. I'm proud of it."

"A wh-wh-whole year?" I was stunned.

"A matter of principle, Susan. Could've been five years. Or even ten. I'm a stubborn man."

He studied Pa's face real close, then began to chuckle. "*You* might even grow a beard one day, Neighbor Wilson."

"Nah. It ain't custom here." Pa shifted on his feet. "It just ain't natural."

"On the contrary. Nothing could be more natural. Well, I'll get back to chopping my wood now. You go right on in."

Pa hesitated then, but I wanted to go in so bad I just ran up those steps without looking back. Wishing, hoping . . . At first there was no sound. Then I heard the most beautiful noise in the world behind me: Pa's heavy boots clumping up the steps.

Louey opened the door for us. She was wearing a long apron. "Morning. My mother's in the kitchen."

She pointed the way and Pa went ahead with his basket, but she held me back a minute to whisper, "You look so pretty. I'm glad you've come. I had a feeling you would today, so I named my doll Queen Susan. She used to stammer, but she doesn't anymore.

"Here." Louey took a black-eyed Susan out of her apron pocket. "Queen Susan is wearing a whole crown of them." She tucked the flower in my hair over my ear.

Then we followed Pa inside to the kitchen, picking our way carefully because it was still one big clutter.

Sister Abigail was kneading dough. She filled a dipper with water and rinsed her hands and then dried them on her apron. "What beautiful corn!" she said. "What perfect lettuce!"

She was very grateful for all the produce.

Pa just grinned. He was good at growing things and proud of it. "I come along with Susan because I want to know what kind of learning she'll get here."

"Of course. You need to speak to my husband. He's arranging books on the new shelves in the common room. I'll get him. Susan, would you like to help Louisa? She is about to wash our lunch apples. I'll go fetch her father."

Louey stood over a big tin tub and began to wash what looked like a whole bushel of apples. I was happy to do the drying with an old yellow towel. "You going to eat all these apples for lunch?" I asked.

She nodded. "Yes. Aren't they lovely? Maybe Marmee will invite you to eat with us."

"New shelves for books," Pa muttered as he looked around. "Books can wait. This old kitchen is what needs the new shelves." He stamped his foot, testing a loose floorboard. "And a floor and a stove and a whole lot of fixing. Never mind the books. You can't eat books."

Louey looked over at him. "How remarkable! That is exactly what Mother said. But Father and Brother Charles insisted on books first. 'We cannot live even a day without our books,' they said, and they argued till Mother gave way."

To me she grumbled softly, "Marmee often gives way even if she's in the right. For Father's sake." She put her finger over her lips. Our first secret.

41

In came her parents. Her father's black suit had been brushed off neatly. "Morning. I'm Brother Bronson." He shook hands with Pa, who introduced himself. "How are you, Susan?"

"Very w-well, sir."

"Won't you both come with me to the common room? You are the very first visitors to see it since we put up a hundred feet of shelving."

We walked behind him into a room that had walls of books. I had not known there were so many books in the whole world. Pictures hung in the few spaces that were not already hidden. The statue of Socrates was there, and there were benches and chairs. A giant bouquet of daisies and cornflowers and wild carrot stood in a china vase on a side desk.

It was a lovely room and made me wish reading aloud was not so hard for me. What a pleasure to go in there and sit down. I wondered if in one of those books there were pictures of Queen Penelope weaving and then sneaking down and unraveling.

"Please sit," our host said. "This is where all of us will congregate to have Conversations and to read and learn."

Pa and I sat down side by side on a wooden bench.

"My wife tells me you are concerned about what Susan will be studying here," the schoolmaster said, seating himself across from us in a rocker.

Pa nodded.

"First, sir, I want to assure you that I am a Christian, and it is my belief that Jesus Christ was the wisest teacher ever to come on earth."

Pa breathed out and relaxed a bit.

"In fact, we are all believers here," he went on, "though some are Come-Outers." He turned to me. "Those are folks who have left the church because it does not condemn slavery." He looked grave.

"P-Pa's agin slavery," I said, proud that he was against this *bad* thing.

"But I go to my church," Pa corrected me real fierce.

"Each man must obey his own conscience," Brother Bronson continued. "I believe that spiritual power runs the world. I use conversation as a teaching method." He nodded at the statue of the old Greek. "Like Socrates here, and Aristotle, and Pythagoras."

"You mean, just plain talking?"

"Exactly. Teaching is a sharing of mind with mind. The child is the book. By talking with children in a clean and beautiful environment, I get them to think and feel and know themselves."

Pa was apparently having trouble taking it all in. For him, school was reading, writing, and arithmetic. Drills. Doing sums. That was how he'd learned. He cracked his knuckles the way he did when he was puzzling over something. "Well, see here. Susan don't talk hardly at all, but she already knows herself. She's been the same Susan Wilson for ten years now. What else will she learn? I mean real learning."

The schoolmaster sighed. "That is my idea of real learning. But we will do mathematics, Latin, French, literature, geometry, and music. And I shall, of course, help her to speak well."

Pa cleared his throat. "That's a tall order. But, let's give it a try. I'm going to speak plain. I don't accept charity. I'll pay with produce from the garden."

The schoolmaster objected. "No payment. We shall be very grateful for your help and your gifts. But they must be gifts. Fruitlands is a spiritual community."

Pa continued. "We Wilsons have been farming here for nigh on fifty years now. We grow more than we need. Maybe I can even help out a little with the farming or work around the place—or give you advice."

"We'd appreciate that. We have come to live here together as brothers because we want nothing to do with payments—with money or commerce."

"How will you buy what you need?" Pa wondered.

"We'll barter our services, or our crops once we have them, and Providence will provide." He smiled sweetly. He stood up, and so did Pa and I. "I believe you've already met Brother Joseph outside."

"Yes," said Pa.

"Well, I should like you to know Brother Charles Lane, too. His thinking, along with mine, brought us here. May we call tomorrow morning?"

"It'd have to be after milking."

"That's fine."

"Susan can find her way home easy enough when lessons are done," Pa said. "No hurry. She's too frail to be much of a help around home, so she can stay as long as she don't get underfoot."

"Th-Th—" I turned my head aside and curled my tongue and silently recited, Out, damned stutter! Out, I say! "Th-Thanks, Pa."

Why did talking to him tie my tongue? He was my own father.

"Study hard and behave. Make your aunt Nell proud." He shook his forefinger at me. "And do your best to speak normal! These folks haven't time for all that stumbling and stammering. Hear what I say?"

I nodded, but this time I kept silent. It would take more than magic to change things with Pa. Nodding was safest with him.

5. Real Schoolmates at Last

The schoolmaster watched Pa move away down the road before he spoke. "Your father mistakes us, Susan. We have all the time in the world at Fruitlands. And what better thing to do than to help you?" He smiled. "So don't worry about your words here. Just say whatever you please."

At that moment, Louey wandered in from the kitchen.

"The other children are all playing in the meadow," her father said. "Suppose you two girls run along out there till I ring the bell."

Down the shaky front steps we dashed to meet them all.

As we came close, we saw them racing about the field, finishing a game of "I Spy," after which they began to collapse one by one on the grass. Their attention turned to the boy, who had begun to climb a large maple tree. He started slow, first one hand up, then a foot, then the other hand. All of a sudden, he was shinnying up the tall trunk, moving faster and faster.

Then he was way up and swinging back and forth from a sturdy branch, happy as a monkey. When he started to swing one-handed, I felt dizzy and couldn't bear to watch. My whole body trembled, so I shut my eyes.

That's the way I kept them—shut tight—for a long time, till I heard his voice real close and I was positive he was down and standing safely on the earth.

Louey, running ahead of me, shouted, "Friends, Romans, countrymen, lend me your ears. I've brought a new schoolmate," and they turned toward us.

When I caught up with her, she named them one by one.

"This is Anna, my older sister, who is twelve. And that is little May whose hand she holds."

Anna had honey brown hair and a very pretty face.

"Since Anna is the eldest, she's usually in charge," Louey continued, "and sometimes she's a little bossy. But mostly she's all right. Anna is going to be a lady and put her hair up and have elegant manners." Louey held up an imaginary teacup, keeping her pinky crooked high, and sipped air.

"Oh, Louisa, hush," Anna chided. From her quiet tone and manner, I could tell she took her responsibility seriously.

"I'm next in age," Louey said, "and there's a great deal to tell about me. I shall be a famous actress and write things that earn trunkfuls of money. And I shall *never* be a young lady. I'm going to be a scapegrace."

"Louisa is a great tease," Anna said fondly. "She doesn't mean it."

"But I do. I do mean it. Next is dear Elizabeth, who is eight and has the best heart in the world. She will give away anything she has. She is the most unselfish of us all."

Anna smiled approvingly at that description, and Elizabeth, who was chubby and rosy, hugged Louisa for her generous words. How lucky they all were to have each other.

"May is almost three and our favorite playmate. And then there's William Lane—from faraway England. He's our age, Susan."

"Call me Willy," the boy said. He was fair-haired with blue eyes and high color in his cheeks. He stepped a pace forward and bowed. "I'm jolly glad to meet you."

I loved the bowing and wished Aunt Nell and Pa would follow the custom, too.

"Do you play draughts?" Willy asked. He spoke his words in the strangest way; I hardly understood him.

"I d-d-don't know."

"Draughts are checkers," Elizabeth explained.

"Oh! Y-y-yes, I play a little."

"Good! And chess?" he asked. He saw my bewilderment.

"I'll teach you. It's a battle game you play on a draught board, and it's fun."

"Susan stammers sometimes," Louey told them, "like Tad used to. But she's going to be cured."

Suddenly she was gone, galloping toward the tree. "My turn to climb!" she shouted.

I couldn't bear to watch.

Luckily Anna spoke to me just then. "I know a remedy for stammering," she said softly.

"L-L-Louisa has already taught me several," I whispered.

Then, to my own surprise, I made the forefinger mustache, stamped my foot, and commanded like King Alfonso: "Begone, vile stammer!"

Anna laughed. "My sister loves words. She thinks they cure everything. I know a silent way." She puckered up her mouth. "Poof!" She blew hard. "Blow, and the stammer will just fly away like dandelion seeds. Will you try it, Susan?"

"Of c-c-c—" I puckered up and blew fiercely. "Of course."

"See?" She laughed gaily.

In my whole life nobody had ever really tried to cure me. Pa just got impatient and scowled when I stammered, and Aunt Nell pretended it wasn't happening.

"That's it," Anna said. "Soon you'll speak beautifully. Practice just blowing the stumbles away."

"Want a turn flying through the air, Susan?" Louey called as she swung back and forth from above.

I looked up for one second. She seemed to know no fear. Her face was glowing with joy.

I studied the ground. Nothing in this whole world could have made me glance up again. "N-n-no, thank you."

I didn't care to tell them all how afeared I was of heights. I was terrified. Always had been.

After a bit, she dropped down lightly and came to me. "How come?"

"I l-l-like to keep my feet on the earth," I explained. "Always."

"You mean you've never, ever, flown?" Louey frowned. "Not once? Even little May here loves swinging on a low bough."

Hearing this, the little girl began to beg, "Let me fly. Louey, let me. Please? Marmee lets me. . . . "

And soon she was hanging bravely from a thick, leafy branch, her sisters hovering very close by. Holding on tight with her two little hands, she was laughing all the while.

She's braver than I am, I thought. I couldn't explain it. I wished I was different. The school bell rang just in time to save me from further talk of climbing trees. How did it happen that I was born scared? And they were born brave?

Across the field and up the shaky steps we ran, passing beneath the Fruitlands sign. And I stepped into another life.

First, Brother Charles Lane, a tall, grim-faced man—
he looked like our preacher—played his violin and we
sang hymns. He played so sweetly, it was surprising that
he looked sour. He instructed us in singing and I thought
our voices golden.

And then we danced.

Even I danced. I took turns with Louey and Anna and
Elizabeth, but I was too shy to dance with Willy; however,
he did not lack partners. I loved dancing.

Brother Charles made pleasant music, but somehow I
couldn't feel at ease with him. He frowned even as he
played happy songs. When he took a turn teaching, he
asked hard questions.

"Susan," he summoned me, "let us have a Conversation."

I went to sit before him.

He was interested in my character. "What is your
worst fault, child?" he asked. As if that one were not hard
enough to answer, he added a second question: "What is
your greatest virtue?"

"I c-c-cannot tell, sir," I said.

"Perhaps you are not accustomed to thinking about
such things," he suggested, not unkindly. "Think on
them. I shall ask you again. One should know one-
self."

Well, I gave those questions a lot of thought, and I
decided that my greatest fault was that I was a coward.

Then I tried to come up with a virtue. I could think of but one! I was quiet, not rowdy. But if my tongue had been quick, I'd have been talking all the time, clucking away like a happy old hen. Gobbling away like a turkey. I don't think I'd ever shut up.

Even as I am now, I say things to myself all day long in my head. I say sacks of things, sacks and bushels and wagonloads. I talk to Pa a lot—silent like that. It's the only way I can, and it makes me feel better.

I couldn't come up with a single other virtue, and I didn't want to admit that to anyone, least of all this strict teacher. What would he think of a ten-year-old without a virtue?

Luckily, he moved on to talk to Anna, and Brother Bronson took a turn with me while our classmates read.

It was a deal easier talking to him. He sat patiently listening and seemed not to notice my stammering. He had no hard questions. He simply was interested in my thoughts this first day.

That was easy—I told him true. "I love the music. I've never d-danced with anyone else before. I shall l-l-learn all the songs. But I d-d-disappointed Brother Charles. I don't know about my virtues and faults."

"Don't you worry about that," he said. "All Brother Charles wants you to be is the best person you can be. He wants that for each one of us. And we all must try for perfection. It is a struggle."

You are perfect already, I thought. You are the kindest man in the world, the best schoolmaster. But, of course, I didn't say it.

"I am so happy to be here," I said, "and I shall c-c-come early each day and d-do all my lessons."

Then I told him my fear: "Louisa and I are the same age, but I'm pr-probably behind her in everything, especially r-reading."

Though I stammered often as my thoughts came tumbling out, he didn't take note of it. Not once. So I didn't let it stop me.

"Never measure yourself by others," he advised. "Perhaps you do not have as much schooling as Louisa. But I am willing to bet you know the countryside with all its secrets and beauties: birds and animals—"

"And caves and f-fresh springs and where the birds n-nest and where the b-b-best b-berries grow," I added in a rush, bobbing my head up and down. This was what I knew most.

"Then you already understand Nature's treasures and can share them with Louisa." He smiled at me. "Will you be her teacher, as she will be yours?"

"Oh, y-y-yes sir. As best I can."

"Good. Write in your diary, Susan, and come to know your own heart. That is the greatest lesson."

We all practiced penmanship and did some geography using a big fat globe with a map of the whole world on it.

The globe turned, and I learned that was the same way the earth moves. It revolves around an imaginary straight line called its axis.

Earth is moving all the time, though we don't feel it. It's moving right now. Louey showed me how to trace faraway Africa and India. She put my finger first on Greece, where Socrates lived and where Queen Penelope did her weaving and unraveling.

Then Willy helped me find Egypt, where Cleopatra ruled. He knew exactly where it was. "Nothing to it," he said. "Now let's twirl the globe and you find it."

"Oh, no," I protested, but too late. He'd already started it spinning.

When it slowed down, I began to look and I found it.

"Jolly good," he said. "I knew you would."

All these places seemed very tiny for such great events to have occurred. But hadn't the American Revolution started at Concord, a really small place near where we lived? We were part of that greatness.

Last, Louey's mother came in while her bread was baking to tell us a true story. "Once, long ago," she started, "certain people right here in Massachusetts—in the town of Salem—came to believe their neighbors, mostly poor old lonely women, were witches, so they arrested them and put them in jail."

She went on to tell how bad their neighbors treated them and how her own ancestor, Samuel Sewall, had been one of the judges at the witch trials in 1692.

Nineteen witches were condemned. *Condemned* means the judges said they should be hanged.

"And they *were* hanged, the whole bunch of them, right on the village green. The townsfolk came out to watch," Sister Abigail said.

I shivered. *I* wouldn't watch. If I had been there, I would have shut my eyes tight.

"I think it was very unfair of them," Louey said, "to pick on old women just because they lived alone with a bunch of cats and didn't have any teeth and were peculiar."

"We all agree with that," Anna said, and we did.

Even Judge Sewall saw it that way, finally—five years after the trials. He was very sorry for his part, but it was too late. That terrible sorrow stayed with him always.

"So every year, on the anniversary of the witch trials," Sister Abigail finished the story, "aged Judge Sewall came a-walking into meeting in the Old South Church in Boston and stood up before the congregation and said, 'I accept the blame and the shame for those convictions and ask pardon.'

"Every year he made this his day of repentance. He fasted and prayed, asking God to forgive him."

This story made me think a lot and I decided that being a judge must be very hard. You give your best opinion, but what if you're wrong? Judge Sewall didn't mean to do harm. He just made a mistake. A big mistake.

"But how could a smart man like him believe his neighbors were witches?" I asked Sister Abigail.

"Because smart men sometimes make mistakes," she said. "Honest mistakes but bad ones."

Even though her story of the witches was heartbreaking, Sister Abigail told it so powerful and real, I was sorry when it was over.

Then lessons ended with the teacher inviting Anna to open the door to the beautiful outside world. A different child each day would have that privilege.

That very first day I asked the others what their favorite subjects were. Elizabeth said she loved music best, and Anna was captured by fine penmanship and history; Willy said he was a wizard in Latin and math, so he loved them best.

I chose story time as my favorite, and Louey agreed with me because she loved to read ghost stories and romances and adventures, all sorts of tales, and then she'd make up her own. Stories and poems and plays let her pretend—let her imagine; they took her far away, farther than any ship or any horse and carriage ever could.

Stories made Louey's mind soar like a falcon, high and swift and graceful.

I understood exactly what she meant. I had lived close to the ground all my life.

Now I wanted my mind to fly, too.

6. Setting the Table
Without Dishes

"You must stay and have lunch with us, Susan, if your aunt won't mind," Sister Abigail said as she worked in her kitchen.

I was glad to accept. "May I help set the table?" I offered.

"There's not much to set. We won't be using dishes," Elizabeth answered gravely. "Everyone just gets a napkin. It saves washing up."

What a wonderful idea! I was learning so much! I mostly do the washing up at home, and I hate it. If I could manage to convince Aunt Nell to just use napkins sometimes, well then . . .

I set myself to watch carefully and see how they worked it. How would we all arrange to take our portions and eat?

One thing I guessed about lunch at Fruitlands: There wouldn't be any soup or stew. Nothing mushy.

Before we sat down, Louey showed me her doll with the crown of black-eyed Susans. "She might learn to swing from branches one day," she said, winking at me. "She might just fly through the air."

"I don't think she ever will, Louey. Not so long as her name is Susan."

She squeezed my hand.

It was an odd lunch indeed. I soon understood why we didn't need dishes. Our old friends, the washed apples, were the main course. Along with fresh bread and water, they were the *whole* lunch.

At table were all the Alcotts, Willy Lane and his father, and Brother Joseph and his beard. The two other members were there as well. First, Brother Everett—who also wore a beard but a tiny one like a fringe on his chin. And finally there was Brother Wood Abram, who was silent. Not one little sentence. Not even "Pass me an apple, please." Not a single word. Not even "Apple."

He just sat there waiting patiently till someone at the table noticed he had no food. Elizabeth, who sat near him, made it her particular job to see that he got his portion. She just smiled sweetly and put bread and apples in front of him. He nodded at her, then ate with his eyes closed.

Anna told me afterward that his name was really Abram Wood. He had a lot of trouble with his family at home about switching it around because he liked it better backward. "Of course," she said, "nobody at Fruitlands minds calling him whatever he likes."

I thought about Pa and what he'd say to that. He'd mind, all right. He'd say when a man is given a name, he ought to stick with it till it gets carved on his tombstone. And folks who humored a man who fooled with his own name were pretty strange critters themselves.

Pa had fixed ideas about most things.

"C-can Wood Abram talk?" I asked Anna.

"Yes, he can talk," she said, "but he almost never does. He believes he is closer to God and his Inner Spirit if he is silent."

"Do you think he's cl-cl-closer?" I asked her. Talking was so hard for me that if God really liked silence best, I might try it myself.

Anna looked thoughtful. "I don't know."

Louey told me a secret about Brother Everett. He had wicked relatives who, a year before, had put him in an insane asylum. "He's really nice," she said indignantly. "He works very hard and he tries to help Marmee with chores." She looked fierce. "His relatives should be put in the asylum!"

Ten years of living with Pa and Aunt Nell had not prepared me for one morning at Fruitlands.

"You are probably wondering at our lunch, Susan," Brother Charles said suddenly.

"N-No sir," I said, wanting to be polite. But it was a dishonest answer. "I mean, yes sir."

"Willy will explain." He nodded at his son.

"An unsoiled body allows an unsoiled spirit to emerge. So our diet is strictly of the pure and bloodless kind," Willy obediently recited.

His father nodded, pleased. "No animal substances, neither flesh, butter, cheese, eggs, nor milk, pollute our table. Neither tea, coffee, molasses, nor rice is taken here. We drink only pure aqua." Picking up another apple from the table, he took a large bite of it. "Mmmm!" he exclaimed. "Ambrosia!"

"There's not so m-much you can ch-choose from to eat then, sir," I said.

Brother Bronson answered me. "On the contrary, Susan. Just think of what grows in the fields, the orchards, and our gardens. Anna will tell you."

"Wheat, rye, barley, maize, oats, buckwheat, apples, pears, peaches, plums, cherries, currants, berries, potatoes, peas, beans, beets, carrots, and melons," Anna listed loyally. "And there is more . . . ."

"Yes," Brother Charles had chewed up his bite of ambrosia-apple and swallowed it, so he joined the talk again. "With so much delicious local produce, we have no need for business and trade and imports. We shall eat what we raise and what grows freely about us. It is an abundance!"

But you are only eating apples and bread and water, I thought. And it was as if Sister Abigail had heard my thought.

"Not is," Sister Abigail corrected him. "It is not an abundance yet. It will be. We must hope it will be an abundance—once the seeds are planted in the ground."

"Faith." Brother Charles's eyes flashed. "One must have faith."

"Once the seeds are planted in the ground," she repeated firmly. "Till our crops grow we must learn to be content with wild salad greens, with dandelions and purslane." She bustled about her chores.

She had baked the bread and provided the meal, and whenever her husband spoke she looked at him pleasantly and listened. She seemed always to find what he said interesting. But other than insisting on the seeds being planted before they all sat around harvesting the crop, she took no part in the talk.

After helping clear up—it took only a few minutes—I said thank you and set off for home. Louey walked me to the rock fence that divided our land from theirs. With Lady Macbeth and King Alfonso helping, we had a long conversation.

"I love your dress," she said. "It makes you look dainty."

"Aunt Nell s-sewed it for me. She's very kind. She's r-raised me ever since I was three weeks old. My ma died of a fever soon after birthing me."

She took my hand, and we went along in the sunshine swinging hands.

"Aunt Nell says I was so tiny when I was n-n-newborn, I was smaller than a corncob doll. She could hold all of me in one hand."

"I would've liked to see you then." Louey grinned. She stopped and measured out a corncob length of air between her hands, and I had to grin, too.

"Aunt loved my mother. P-P-Pa did, too. Thing is, he never seemed to get over her d-dying. Maybe because he was a good bit older than she was when they married, he n-n-never could figure out how she could go and die so young. It just didn't seem right."

"It wasn't right," Louey said. "It was wrong!" That was a strong way to talk about what the good Lord did. I pressed her hand hard in gratitude.

We were at the fence, our parting place, but I had to go on talking.

"I love my mother too, even though I never knew her. She gave me my name. I'll tell you a secret. Because it's her gift to me, I'll never have a nickname. Not Sue or Susie. Not anything but Susan because I treasure it."

Louey said, "You're right. Susan is a beautiful name."

"Sometimes I go with Aunt Nell to the churchyard and lay bouquets of black-eyed Susans on her grave," I finished up.

"I'll go with you one day if you'll let me," Louey promised. "Now I better head back home. See you tomorrow."

I watched her till she was out of sight.

Oh, how my aunt questioned me about all I'd learned. First, she needed to know whether they wore shoes all the time. That was information for Pa. When I began telling her about lunch without dishes, she was surprised. "No forks? No plates? How'd they drink their water?"

"Oh, they have gl-glasses. They do have plates and t-tableware, too. They just weren't using them. They were saving work."

That seemed to make sense to her.

Well, when she told Pa, he was considerable pleased about the shoes. But he was scandalized about the way lunch was served.

"I never heard tell of such a thing," he said, "'cept among savages. Cannibals."

"Henry. They're vegetarians," Aunt Nell reminded him. "What's the harm? Lord knows there's times when I wish we didn't use dishes. The newcomers seem like real good folks to me. Won't even hurt an animal. So how could they hurt our Susan?"

He couldn't think of a way.

"Look, she's got color in her cheeks." Aunt Nell smiled at me. "Did you children play outdoors?"

I nodded. "Tag and a lot of r-r-running around and stuff."

I left out the tree climbing. I hadn't done it anyway.

"Louey—the girl we met first visit—is my age. She's very nice. She wr-writes poems and stories and makes up plays."

Aunt Nell looked impressed.

I didn't tell about being best friends and sharing secrets. I kept that to myself.

"I'm glad," Aunt Nell said. "They're nice neighbors. It's lucky that they've moved here."

"Well, we'll know about that soon enough," Pa said.

"How's that, Henry?"

"They're coming to visit early tomorrow morning."

"Tomorrow morning? Heavens, we've got chores to do...." Aunt Nell said. Nobody ever came a-visiting us early on a weekday morning.

"I know. It ain't Sunday, but the two dreamers who dreamed up paradise next door got time for visiting. I warned them to come after milking time. They don't seem to know that 'Man goeth forth unto his work and to his labour until the evening.' I'll just hear 'em out. Then we'll have to see what's what. I have my doubts about this schooling." Pa frowned.

"Oh, Henry," Aunt Nell protested, "learning can't harm a child. Give it a chance."

"Well, Nell, just you remember. In this house, we eat our food on dishes and we all wear shoes. We are civilized folk!"

So are they, Pa, I thought disloyally. I think I like their civilization better.

Dear Diary,

Today was my first day of lessons at Fruitlands. The Consociates are odd folk but very nice to me. Nobody minds that I stammer or even corrects me or prompts me. They just let me find my word. It's amazing. It loosens my tongue.

Brother Charles is very severe. I do not think I shall like him. That is wicked but it is true.

The Consociates talk a lot about seeking the Inner Spirit and the True Self. They all want to be better people. I would like to be better, too. But bread and apples and water wouldn't do it for me. They would just make me hungrier for stew and chicken.

Does eating meat turn you into a wicked person? 'Cause my folks eat meat and they aren't wicked.

What makes a person bad? Is Brother Abram Wood a better person because he does not talk and he calls himself Brother Wood Abram?

Brother Charles should play the violin more and think less. The violin is sweet. Thinking too much makes him sour.

Willy Lane calls checkers draughts and says he'll teach me how to play chess. I never thought a boy would be my friend.

I pray Pa will let me continue.

I believe these are my true and honest thoughts and they belong in a diary.

7. A Little Pitcher with Giant Ears

I needed to bring my new friends a present. Right off they'd given me a diary and my schooling and lunch. Pa's giving garden vegetables to Fruitlands reminded me that if I was going to take, I had to give in return. Give what? I didn't own anything.

I worried and fretted about it. Then I recalled what the schoolmaster had said about Nature.

Rising at sunup, I quietly took a clean quart jar from Aunt's pantry and, after putting grass in it, went out to her rosebushes and began to collect the ladybugs that sat all over the blossoms and leaves like yellow-speckled jewels.

I brushed them in so gentle, not a one got hurt. I gathered so many bugs, the jar was just bursting with them, and I covered the top with a cheesecloth so they'd live. Then I hid the jar outside behind a rock and ran in to have my breakfast.

Brother Bronson and Brother Charles were there sitting opposite Pa at the far end of the kitchen table, refusing all Aunt Nell's good food and drink. They would take only water. "Water is Nature's champagne," said Brother Charles. "Don't you agree it is Mother Nature's wine?" He looked to the schoolmaster, who nodded.

Aunt Nell gave 'em each a frosty glass of Mother Nature's wine from our well, then fetched my porridge and milk and sat down by the hearth to shell peas.

"I could send my girl to eat in the other room," Pa suggested. "Little pitchers have big ears."

"Please don't," Brother Bronson said. "Children should be included in all discussions. They learn much that way."

"Even when it don't concern them?"

"What concerns us also concerns them. They are simply younger versions of us, perhaps more perfect than we."

I know Pa didn't think I was perfect, but he let me stay.

They were arguing about farming. Seems the Consociates were going to farm only with hand tools. "It's foolish," Pa argued. "You need animals to pull the plow, and you must fertilize that poor land with manure."

Brother Charles wrinkled up his nose like that manure was right there on Aunt Nell's spotless kitchen table. "No subjugation of animals. No animal fertilizers," he ruled. "We shall enrich the land with the return of its own fresh green crops—with vegetable mulch."

"You got to grow crops afore you can plow them under," Pa pointed out, and he went on till it looked to me like he was winning the schoolmaster around.

But Brother Charles suddenly put up his hand and said, *"No. No animals. No manure."* He didn't give the schoolmaster enough chance to make up his own mind.

I could tell who would win whenever they disagreed—Brother Charles. He seemed to start out knowing he was right and didn't give way.

I listened to snatches of the farming talk as I ate. Mostly I was thinking about my beautiful ladybugs and how baby May, especially, would love them; how she would laugh. When May laughed it was like music, it made everyone happy. Even Wood Abram smiled.

Brother Bronson changed the subject. "I hope to plant an orchard of fruit trees, and I've set aside a corner near the house for mulberry trees as well."

"Fruit trees are a good idea. But nobody round these parts grows mulberry trees. Why?" Pa inquired.

Brother Charles answered. "Because of our community's ideals that neither man nor beast should be used or sacrificed for another's benefit."

"I don't follow."

"The mulberry trees will help us solve the problem of clothing. Since we cannot wear cotton because it is raised with slave labor, or wool which deprives the sheep of their coats, then we have only linen. We need to vary it and will do it with silk. So my mulberry trees will be for silk-worms," Brother Bronson said, pleased.

"You don't say," said Pa. "It still ain't quite clear to me what you're all aiming for."

Now I paid attention because I wanted to know, too.

Pa ticked the points off on his fingers. "You want to live together and share. You don't want to hurt man nor beast. And you don't care about money and profit. All very worthy Christian aims. But farming's hard work. How will you divide up the labor?"

"Each of us will choose the chores best suited to him," Brother Charles answered. "No person shall be demeaned by what he does."

Aunt Nell spoke up. "Who will want to do all the mean daily chores like housecleaning and washing up and cooking?"

It's not a matter of choosing, Aunt, I thought. Sister Abigail just got stuck with all the work. Because she's a woman. Louey says men think women like to do the household chores, but really they'd rather be reading, she says, or dancing or eating *bonbons*, which are little French chocolates. Oh, I could have answered Aunt's question. But I just filled my mouth with porridge and listened to the schoolmaster's words.

Funny, he understood everything in the world except this.

"My wife has taken charge of all the womanly tasks," he said confidently. "She is a wonderful manager. They are simple chores to her."

God transformed Aunt Nell into His butterfingered handmaiden again right then. Onto the stone hearth she dropped the colander with a fearful clatter. "Excuse me," she said. "That was plumb clumsy of me."

Now, Aunt Nell was not clumsy. I tipped my head in her direction to listen close. Sure enough, the clatter was followed by a powerful sniff. She was mad again, but this time not at Pa.

"My wife is devoted to home and family," the schoolmaster continued. "And the girls will help her. We hope other female Consociates will join us later on."

"All right." Pa scratched the back of his head. "Tell me this. Who—" he leaned forward on the table with genuine interest, "will want to do all the mean, heavy, dirty chores, the tiring work outdoors? Farming ain't no picnic."

"We shall find means to accomplish all."

"How?" Pa wouldn't let up.

"Through the Spirit," Brother Charles said. "Man is more than flesh. We shall persevere through the Spirit."

The two guests rose. "We hope you will visit us and give us the benefit of your wisdom," Brother Bronson said as he took his leave.

"Thank you," Pa said. "We will see."

"In the evenings," Brother Bronson continued, "when work is done, we meet to think. We have Conversations. And we join together in evensong. You and Miss Wilson are welcome. And Susan, too, anytime."

Pa stood in the kitchen doorway, watching the two men start down the path. "The Lord help you," he muttered. "You're sure going to need all His help. And then some."

"Sister Abigail is the one who really needs the help," Aunt Nell corrected him sharply. "Peculiar cooking on a rickety old stove for eleven people. No cheese, no meat— in that old kitchen. And all the other work besides? Pshaw." She gave a double sniff. "Paradise? Huh. Maybe it's a man's idea of paradise. To me it sounds closer to the Other Place." She pointed down. "One woman can't do all that work. And shouldn't have to."

Then she turned to me quick as if she'd said too much. "If you're finished with breakfast, go along with them for schooling, child."

"They'd better be good schoolteachers," Pa said, "because they sure ain't good farmers."

"They're wonderful schoolteachers," I said, running to pick up my treasure in the jar and to catch up with the

Fruitlanders. I didn't want to hear another word my folks had to say. I suspected it would be a disagreeable conversation. I really didn't want to know, because, peculiar as they were, I liked the Fruitlanders. Who wants to hear bad talk about friends?

"I'm afraid the children must do without music this morning while you take your turn in the field," Brother Bronson was saying when I caught up with them. "We need to finish so we can plant our grain."

"Yes, I suppose so," Brother Charles agreed, "though I have some thinking to do. Still . . . "

They quickened their steps, and soon I saw my friends in the meadow. I hid my bugs under some blueberry bushes and watched my schoolmates in the glorious morning sunlight as they took turns climbing up trees and swinging from branches.

Willy, don't break your neck afore I beat you in checkers! my mind screamed. Why don't you just stay safe on the ground near me? I bit my tongue to keep from crying out warnings: *Stop! Be careful! Hold on tight! Come back down!*

Anna and Elizabeth stayed low and swung quietly. I could watch them without my heart racing with fear. May's little feet almost scraped the ground. She held on tightly and drifted back and forth happily.

I could have swung on a low branch, like May did, my toes dragging along the earth. That wasn't really swinging.

But any higher? I always had this fear that a strong wind might suddenly blow me up and away. Or, worse, loosen my hands and I'd fall . . . .

I peeked through one slightly opened eye, and I saw Louey gliding perilously high—almost to the sun it seemed.

What would it be like to be brave? To float overhead, to sail through the air and be kissed by the breezes? I was unable to imagine such freedom and wished my friends were down safe with their feet on the ground.

When Louey finally landed breathless beside me, laughing, she asked me, "How about it, Susan? Want to try? Want to take one turn being an eagle?"

I shook my head. "No thank you. I l-like to keep my f-feet close to the grass."

She looked disappointed. "I could teach you to swing real low, holding on with only your knees."

"Louisa," Anna said, "you may not do that or I'll have to tell Marmee." Louey didn't argue. I guess she was a bit ashamed of teasing.

"I brought a surprise," I said. "It's hid till playtime."

"Oh, tell, tell!" everyone begged. "Give us a hint!" But I wouldn't. Louey was especially excited. "I love surprises better than anything!" she exclaimed.

Inside, we lacked Brother Charles and his violin because he was in the fields working. But school was lovely, even though we couldn't start the day with dancing. Brother Bronson taught so wonderfully. He could make any subject—even nouns and verbs—interesting.

"Gymnastic spelling," he announced, "so that baby May can learn how to do her letters." Then he began to act out each letter. He crossed his arms for *X* and walked stiffly across the room for *I* and rounded his back for *C* and made a true *F* with his two arms outstretched left, one above the other. For *S* he curved his head and chest forward and bent his knees so that he managed to turn himself into an actual *S*, all the while also making the hissing sound of a goose so that May would know the letter and the sound together.

What fun to watch living letters. And May was already trying to form letters with crayons on paper. So the early hours flew by.

At playtime, I ran and found my surprise and brought it to where everyone was waiting. "Ladybugs," I said. "I brought you all I could find."

"Must be a quadrillion," Willy said in awe. "I didn't know there were so many in the world."

"They're beautiful. What shall we do with them?" Louey asked.

"Oh, Susan, don't let us hurt them," Elizabeth said, worried.

"Never," I said. "I like to wear them. If you are very gentle and careful, they'll cling to your clothes like speckled beads."

We formed a circle sitting cross-legged on the grass, and I lifted the cheesecloth and tilted the jar to my blouse. A cluster of bugs clung like a glittering brooch. Then I passed the jar to Louey, and so it went round the circle several times till we all had sleeves and blouses beautifully bug-beaded.

Some ladybugs flew away, but most stayed. Nobody, not even May, made a sound, so as not to scare them. Willy tried a few in his hair and then one on his nose. That made us want to laugh, but we bit our lips to stay quiet. May truly loved the ladybugs, so we ended up putting them all over her clothes and her hair, and she became a delightful twinkling Princess Ladybug in the bright sunlight.

When the school bell sounded, I said, "Let's send them all home now," and repeated the little verse Aunt Nell had taught me:

> *"Ladybug, ladybug, fly away home,*
> *Your house is on fire, and your children will burn."*

Then they all recited it—even May—and, flapping our arms and twirling, we sent the bugs flying. We inspected each other carefully to be sure no bugs were trapped in hair or clothes.

"A salute for Susan and her grand surprise," Louey said. "Hip hip hooray." The others joined in. I didn't know where to look; it was the first cheer of my whole life.

We returned to our studies till at noon, the schoolmaster said, "Susan, will you open the door to the beautiful world outside?"

Happily, I ran to do it, but when I looked out I couldn't believe what I saw: Brother Joseph in the field, plowing with a team. Brother Everett was working alongside him, hauling away big rocks. Brother Charles was nowhere in sight. I blinked and looked again. There they were. "S-S-Sir," I said, "there are *animals* working outside in the field."

He smiled. "Not at Fruitlands, Susan. You heard us explain that to your father this morning." He was busy gathering up papers and books, but he came to the doorway. "At Fruitlands? What is this? What ever can have happened? Come along, children. Let us see."

So we all trailed behind him.

"It can't be done by hand," Brother Joseph said calmly in answer to his question. "You know that as well as I do. We need to plant quickly. We're already late. We'll starve this winter if we don't have these crops. So I just borrowed this team from my family's farm. My wife and brothers said they could spare it. Later on, we'll see. But for now—"

"Where's Brother Charles?"

"He labored for a while. Then he wrenched his back, so he's resting now. Sister Abigail is giving him cold compresses. Two hours digging by hand showed him the folly of it."

"Perhaps it's good that you've brought a team," Brother Bronson said, walking around the animals to inspect them. "But one thing puzzles me. Why not a pair of oxen? Why did you bring an ox and a cow?"

Brother Joseph looked him in the eye. "I can't work hard and live on apples. I'll drink the milk if no one else will. I'll drink it privately in the barn, but I need it for strength."

The schoolmaster seemed sad on hearing that his Consociate was going to drink milk! That same way was how Pa seemed when he heard some member of our church was taking whiskey.

There was a long silence.

"That you drink milk is a matter for your own conscience," Brother Bronson said, and the two men shook hands heartily.

Now, since Aunt Nell always said milk was nourishing, and I had to drink lots of it to be healthy, I was confused. Why should drinking the healthful food be a matter of conscience for a man who was trying to be perfect? A man who spent a whole year in jail fighting to keep his beard because he believed in justice? These new neighbors were just not ordinary folk. They were a constant puzzlement.

There was only one thing for me to do. I'd have to listen very carefully.

I made up my mind I'd start stretching my ears every night. Ten hard pulls on each ear till they were bigger. Till they were big enough.

In order to be smart and really understand, I'd have to be a Little Pitcher with Giant Ears.

8. Brother Charles Attacks the Lamps

Willy beat me at checkers three times running. "I'll show you some strategies," he offered, "and pretty soon you'll be jolly good."

I shook my head.

"Don't be silly, Susan. Once you know how, you'll trounce me." Then he took out a box of tiny carved wooden chess pieces: knights, pawns, castles, kings, and queens. He set them up on the board and began to explain the game, but it was very complicated.

"I don't th-think I can learn," I said when it was my turn to begin. I closed my eyes.

"You don't have to talk in draughts or chess," he said firmly. "They are not hard games. Once you learn the chess moves, I will lend you the pieces so that you can practice. Louisa and Anna and Elizabeth all play. Never say you can't do a thing till you've really tried." He sounded like his pa. "Now, carry on!"

"What?" I opened my eyes.

"Carry on. Continue. Your move."

With trembling fingers I moved one of my pieces.

"Pawn to king four," Willy said. "Good show!" He was pleased.

"Why do you speak so strange?" I asked. "You and your pa both?"

"Everyone in England speaks this way. It's you Americans who speak oddly."

I would've disagreed, 'cepting he was so nice to me. The idea of a whole country speaking English his way was remarkable. I liked chess and made up my mind to try to learn it. I would always call my king King Alfonso.

Because of Fruitlands, each day was better than the day before. Every morning that I set off from home was an adventure. With real friends.

Some school days started with singing and dancing. Others began with gymnastic spelling. When Brother Charles and Brother Bronson were away traveling— holding Conversations about their ideas and looking to recruit new Consociates—Sister Abigail would lead the lessons and tell us fine stories. Anna, who had very grown-up manners, would help.

The one hard thing about schooling was reading out loud. I did just fine reading quietly to myself, but I hated reading out loud. When I read silently, even if I didn't know many words, I could figure out meanings from the sentences. I was good at that. If I had three or four words in a sentence, I got the meaning. But out loud I was slow and halting and got stuck, huffing and puffing, like an ox plowing through rocks.

One morning I burst into tears right in the middle of my reading. Brother Bronson called me to him. He stood with his hands behind his back. "I have a gift for you," he said, and he handed me a small book.

I didn't want that book, any more than I wanted a handful of poison sumac. Even less.

I glanced at the cover: *The Vicar of Wakefield* by Oliver Goldsmith. On the cover was a picture of an odd-looking boy carrying a whole load of green spectacles.

"Louisa is just starting to read this and she loves it," he said. "You will, too. Perhaps she can listen to you read and give you a boost here and there. After a while you'll like doing it. Will you at least try?"

He could not ask anything of me that I would not do. "Yes. Th-Thank you for the book."

Louey loved the idea. Being daughter to a schoolmaster made her itch to try her hand at teaching, I guess. "We'll be a reading club," she said. "After lessons, you can take me to your favorite places, Susan, and we'll carry books. We'll call ourselves the Rambling Readers. Will you join the club, Susan?"

"Oh, yes!" I said. "You can be president."

"For this book. You'll be president for the next one."

Me, president!

On our walks, I would pick up Indian arrowheads or spear tips. I knew the woods and the fields so well, my eyes were keen at sighting interesting objects on the ground. We played at being Indian scouts. Louey said, who cared that Indians never let girls be scouts? Not us.

I showed her how to sit so still in a glade, the squirrels and possums and raccoons would come right up to her and let her pet them. One afternoon as she sat motionless in the sunlight waiting for friendly animals, I noticed a large skunk sneaking along in the tall grass behind her and heading straight for some petting.

Noiselessly, I moved right in front of her. I held my nose and made a terrible face as I pointed over her shoulder. Then I grabbed her hand and we took off for the woods, she running right beside me, the two of us laughing till we could hardly make our feet go. We collapsed on the ground then, safe and still sweet smelling.

One day I spotted an especially interesting broken Indian arrowhead in the grass. She said, "You'll have to meet Father's friend, Mr. Thoreau, when he comes to visit. He knows all about the Indians and plants and animals and insects. Even snakes."

"I sh-should like to meet him," I said.

Louey's two cures didn't work altogether, but they helped a lot. And Anna's helped too. Maybe because folks were talking to me so much—all except Wood Abram; I never did hear him say one word—and I was learning to answer comfortable and easy. At home, I hardly got to say much—nobody did—but at Fruitlands, talking was what the menfolks did most of the time. And what Brother Charles liked to do best.

Louey and I watched fish swim in the river and frogs jump about and splash on the lily pads in the pond.

I taught her how to make a grass whistle by pulling a thick blade of grass between her two thumbs and then blowing on it till it vibrated with a lovely sound. She learned fast and loved playing her tootle—her word for it.

"You know such wonderful things," she said. "Who would think that a piece of grass could be a musical instrument?"

Together we made music.

We were playing *duets*, Louey said.

A duet is music made by two instruments; then there's a trio for three and a quartet for four, and a quintet and a sextet. I guess it goes on and on. I wondered what the word was for a dozen instruments.

Maybe a girl doesn't have to know these things. But I loved knowing them.

The folks at Fruitlands believed the more everyone knew the better they—and the world—would be. In my heart, I was almost becoming a Fruitlander. Except as far as eating was concerned.

When Louey and I rested during our wanderings outdoors, the Rambling Readers Club would come to order and we would read from *The Vicar*. The story was all about the Primrose family, two girls and six boys and their mother and father. The boy carrying all the green spectacles was Moses Primrose, who was very foolish.

I would often stammer or stumble over words. Since Louey knew all the words in the whole world, she would help me. She could mostly guess the word I was stuck on without looking at the book. Reading did get a bit easier, but ever so slowly, very slowly. It was a chore.

I liked *listening* to a good reader.

Folks at Fruitlands read aloud to one another every chance they got. Like after dinner instead of sweets for dessert, they read. Louey, too.

Better than reading, Louey and I acted out parts of the book. I liked best being silly Moses Primrose.

Sometimes Louey made up little plays herself in which each of us could be anybody: a villain with a dagger who was defeated by the brave hero; a lost princess miraculously found by her grieving mother; heartbroken, separated lovers reunited at last.

Once she turned us into slaves escaping from an owner who whipped us. We carried Louey's doll wrapped in a blanket, and as we crept along in darkness, brave but scared, we whispered over and over to one another, "To freedom?"

"Yes, to freedom."

My favorite Louey play, which I asked to do again and again, was the one where a sorceress brewed a magic potion that melted a hardhearted father's heart, so he recognized his true and loving daughter.

But best of all, Louey enjoyed acting out bits of her father's favorite book, *Pilgrim's Progress*. Since she loved the character of Christian, the good man, I got to be ever so many other people: Christiana, his wife; and Greatheart, Hopeful, Giant Despair, and even the foul fiend Apollyon.

It was a wonder how Christian hoped and struggled and overcame monsters and suffered! Then he and Christiana finally succeeded and were reunited. What a happy ending!

Louey and I spent magical hours living their stories out loud.

Sometimes Elizabeth would come with us and we voted her into our secret club; she was a good reader and a wonderful actress. She tied a black shawl over her head and stood all bent over leaning on a stick as she played an old woman of Salem accused of being a witch. "I am innocent," she pleaded softly. "I have done nothing wrong. It is true I have thirteen cats, but they are all the family I have."

I wept. "Don't hang her," I begged Louey, who was the judge. "Please don't."

Of course, Louey let her go and gave her back her farm and all her cats and punished her accusers. She sentenced all of them to be hanged: all the village elders of Salem.

When I acted someone else's life, I didn't stammer.

As time passed, Louey began to tell me more private things that bothered her. Secrets. I was the only one she could talk to about Fruitlands.

"How can a girl who lives in paradise complain to the others who live there?" she asked me. "Paradise is supposed to be a perfect place."

I couldn't answer.

"It bothers me," she admitted, "that Anna is always ladylike and good, and I am often naughty. It shouldn't bother me because Anna is really good. But it does. I'm jealous."

"I'm jealous sometimes, too, Louey. I'm even a little jealous of you because you have a mother and sisters."

"But Anna can't help being good."

"And it's not your fault I don't have a mother."

She thought about it. "Jealousy is not sensible," she decided, and I knew she was right.

She worried about her mother a lot. "Marmee works too hard. It's just not fair."

I agreed, but I couldn't think of anything that would help.

I didn't have so many secrets. I did tell her my worst one the day she and I gathered a bouquet of black-eyed Susans and went to Ma's grave. We cleared the brush and twigs that were lying around and made the whole place neat, then we put the flowers on the grass before the stone marker.

Louey kneeled down near the stone. "Susan Wilson," she read out loud, "1806 to 1832. Rest in Peace." She turned and drew me close by her. She raised her hands in front of her as if in prayer. "I'm Susan's best friend," she said softly, to Ma, "and I'm glad to meet you. Susan misses you."

I was sure Ma heard.

When we were walking home, I spoke about what was so much my mind. "I believe Pa d-d-doesn't really like me, Louey."

"That can't be," she answered quickly.

"He doesn't c-care to look straight at me. He never c-calls me by name or t-talks to me direct. Just through Aunt Nell. And he h-h-hates when I have trouble speaking."

"You're so nice, Susan. It can't be you. It's just his way. Grown-ups are sometimes very odd."

That comforted me a bit though I still wasn't sure about Pa. Certainly Louey knew about odd grown-ups.

One secret that troubled her—and me too—concerned Willy. His father controlled him.

"It's not fair," Louey said. "The Consociates believe in independence, but Willy must always please his father. What he eats, wears, studies, reads—everything he does—is decided by his father."

"I-I've thought about that," I admitted. "One day when Willy was teaching me chess, he suddenly stood up and, looking fierce, raised his fist to the sky. 'I shall grow a beard longer and thicker than Brother Joseph's,' he pledged to the clouds. 'I shall eat sweets and do just as I please when I am grown no matter what Father thinks.' He stamped his foot hard. Then he came back and sat down, and we played as if I had not heard him."

Louey looked impressed.

"Brother Charles is a h-harder father to have, I th-think, than my own pa," I finished.

She nodded.

In fact, many of Louey's secrets were about Willy's father, whose favorite saying was, "I believe in being rather than doing."

I heard him say it at least fifty times.

"I wonder if *being* is what Pa calls idling," I guessed.

"Well, not exactly. He's . . . thinking," she said.

He and the schoolmaster were the chief thinkers at Fruitlands. But they thought very differently: The schoolmaster mixed being with doing. He worked all the time, farming and doing carpentry and pruning trees. He chopped wood and baked bread. He taught us regular. He was always busy and he thought right along with his busyness. But not Brother Charles.

"When Brother Charles starts thinking," Louey warned, "he's dangerous! Whoa! You had better look out!"

The very next day during school, Brother Charles was sitting very quiet at first, and then I saw exactly what Louey meant. He attacked the oil lamps. We were all doing arithmetic in the common room when he rose up suddenly and said to the schoolmaster, "We must not rob the whale!" How he came to be worrying about whales while we were working out how much four times eight is, I don't know. And as for robbing anything, why, there wasn't as much as a crawfish around, much less a whale.

"Candles will have to do for light," he went on. "It's not fair to pillage the leviathan of its oil so that we might selfishly extend the daylight."

Louey's father rubbed his cheek and reflected but didn't answer. He always worried every question a long time, trying to get to a true answer. While he was working on the question, Brother Charles was moving right ahead, wrapping his own answer up tight and tying it in a knot.

He turned to us children.

"Is it fair to rob the whales, Anna?"

"No sir."

"Louisa?"

"Well . . . no sir."

"Elizabeth?"

"No sir."

"Susan?"

"No sir."

Even little May had a turn.

And, of course, Willy.

"Pater," Willy answered bravely, "it will be hard to read in the evening without lamps."

"And so, you would destroy God's mighty leviathan?" His father looked at him sternly.

"No sir."

Meanwhile, the schoolmaster was still weighing the question.

Immediately, Brother Charles started collecting the lamps. "Come along, Willy," he called, and Willy went reluctantly behind him through the rooms, gathering them up.

We all trooped after them, watching.

Into the kitchen they went last, where Brother Charles explained to a surprised Sister Abigail, "We are collecting all the lamps. We shall use only candles after this. It is not fair to the whales to rob them of their oil, is it?"

At first, Sister Abigail just plumb stared at him and did not answer. Slowly, her face reddened and she frowned. "I do not think I can manage with candles," she said after a bit.

"We will use pine knots when absolutely necessary."

Sister Abigail did not give ground. "My eyesight is quite poor, and I do much close work at night."

"Even so, our life here at Fruitlands may require personal sacrifice for the universal good."

The lamp collector looked from her to her husband. He expected support.

But Brother Bronson was still considering the question. He seemed uncomfortable, as if he didn't know which side to take. He did love and care for the animals, and he also loved and cared for his wife. It was a *dilemma*, a word I had newly learned: a problem that has no good solution.

Finally he decided. "Abba dear, let us try it this way. Brother Charles is certainly correct about the whales. What right have we? Let us see how it works out and trust to Providence."

Sister Abigail looked miserable as she watched her lamp disappear down the hall.

Afterward, Louey was very upset. "Mother will miss the lamp terribly. She sews evenings, and late night is the only chance she has to read."

"Why didn't your father stop him?" I asked.

"Brother Charles has Father mesmerized."

"What's that?"

"It's like being under a magic spell. Brother Charles gets Father to do whatever he wants. Father is so eager to devote his life to God and mankind and to be good and pure that he follows Brother Charles."

I knew Louey was right, but what could we do? It was up to her pa to notice that paradise wasn't fair to Sister Abigail.

"My mother has opinions and likes to speak up, but mostly she's too busy washing, cooking, sewing, baking, and doing all the chores," Louey said. "She hasn't even time to talk."

"I always thought it was natural for women to be busy with chores. My aunt Nell works from morning till night. But in paradise Sister Abigail works harder even than Aunt Nell!"

Louey nodded. "Father and Brother Everett help her some, and my sisters and I brush the hearth and sweep the steps and carry the kindling and the water."

And often the sisters tidied up the common room, and every day they picked fresh flowers, and on wash days they pitched in.

"Marmee keeps wishing that some more women will become Consociates," she confided. "They can share the work and be company for her, too."

"My aunt Nell thinks your mother has way too much to do, Louey."

"My mother agrees."

"So why does she do it all?"

Louey looked very solemn. "She does it for Father. She loves him, and he believes in the Newness. As long as he believes, she'll support him."

The *Newness*. I'd heard the word a thousand times at Fruitlands. And even though I was faithfully stretching my ears till they ached each night and listening eagerly to every word spoken near me, I still had no clear idea what it meant.

9. The Great Fruitlands Mystery

I got nowhere trying to figure out the *Newness* for myself. At the week's end, when the men were finally sowing the grain, I got my chance to learn.

"Today's an important day," Louey's father announced once lessons were finished. "We're going to plant the grain for next winter. Louisa?" He smiled. It was time to open the door.

"Let's not have a Ramblers meeting today," Louey whispered hastily. "Let's watch the planting."

So we went to the field and sat on top of the rock fence and watched four of the brothers—Bronson, Wood, Charles, and Everett—preparing to plant. At least they said that was what they were doing. There they all stood, except they weren't sowing anything. They were just talking. Now, Pa had planted his crops long afore this, so I knew they ought to be out there hustling, but they weren't.

"What do they talk about all the time?" I asked Louey.

"What they believe in. The Newness. It has a much longer name: Transcendentalism. But it means Newness."

"What is it?"

She narrowed her eyes and thought for a while. "It's hard to explain. That's why they need to talk about it so much." She stopped and seemed to be sorting it all out in her head. "It means believing that each person has a Spirit inside him."

Speaking slowly and carefully, she continued. "The Consociates think that each person is born with a little voice inside to guide him correctly, an Inner Spirit—and if you just listen closely to your Inner Spirit, you will be a kind, happy person."

"But the little voice inside me sometimes tells me to do naughty things."

"I do naughty things too, Susan. I have a temper. I am impatient and moody. Father says I have to try to listen more closely for my true inner voice. I guess you should, too."

"Does your mother believe in the Newness?"

"I don't think so. Not like the others. But she believes in Father and follows him because she loves him."

"Does she follow Brother Charles, too?"

Louey shook her head. "Not really. Marmee says he doesn't take any joy in life." Her voice dropped to a whisper. "He leads Father more and more. He dominates him."

While we sat up on the rock wall thinking about it, the men who were out to do the planting had sat down right there in the field with their bags of seed around them. They were still talking.

"Brother Charles is always trying to figure out ways for us to get closer to our Inner Spirits."

"Like taking away the lamps?"

"Exactly. Living a pure life is why he and Father started Fruitlands. That's why we're here."

"Worrying more about whales than about your mother doesn't seem so pure to me."

"Susan, you're wicked." Louey giggled. "But I agree."

"What other ways did he think up?"

"Getting up at five each morning and having a cold bath."

The cold bath part was interesting. The only reason we bathed at home was to wash the dirt off us. I never thought a bath had to do anything more.

"Aunt Nell always warms my bathwater," I told Louey. "I don't favor dipping into cold water."

"A cold bath can make you feel radiant!" she said.

"I believe it might just make me feel cold. Are there more ways to get close to the Inner Spirit?"

"Oh, Brother Charles is forever thinking up new ones. Mostly hard ones about eating. We were vegetarians before he and Willy came to live with us, but we ate cheese and milk and molasses in those days—lots of different foods— till he figured out they were all bad for our Inner Spirits."

"My aunt says milk is nourishing. How can it be bad?"

"It robs the cow."

"What if the cow has no calf to drink the milk?"

"I asked him that once," Louey said. "His answer was, 'No matter what, we have no right to the milk.'"

"I guess my folks won't ever hear their Inner Spirits, Louey. They don't ever think about any of this."

"You can never tell," she said. "Father and Brother Charles are still working it all out, and things change. Like tea. Marmee used to love her cup of tea. Then they decided tea was not acceptable. Now all Marmee gets to drink is cold water. She misses her hot tea."

"Brother Charles loves cold water. He calls it champagne."

Louey screwed up her face something awful.

"Don't you ever have sweets?" I asked.

"Never."

I was about to say there can't be a paradise without candy when I noticed the men moving about in the field. Each man had risen and gone to a different corner, and each of them began sprinkling seeds around. "Look, they're planting at last."

We sat there watching them walk and scatter seeds, enjoying the idea that the grain would soon be growing.

Suddenly Louey's father stopped dead in his tracks. He scratched his head. He looked troubled. He went to talk to Brother Charles, and then they called to the other two to stop and join them.

There was a long conference, but this time they didn't sit down. Each one of the sowers went back to his corner and took a handful of seeds out of his bag and carried it back, and then they talked some more and studied the seeds and talked again.

Something was wrong.

"What ever is the matter?" I wondered. It had taken them so long to get started, and now they'd stopped halfway through. Once Pa starts planting, he never stops. Sometimes he ends up working by moonlight, calling Aunt Nell out, too, to get it all done.

"Maybe they need help," Louey said, so we climbed down off the rocks and ran over.

Before we reached them, they seemed to have solved their problem because Brother Everett began to laugh. Then Brother Wood actually grinned, though he didn't make a sound, and even Brother Charles was smiling, sort of, something I didn't think was possible. Brother Bronson looked unsure. Brother Everett was bent over, coughing, when we got to them.

"What's happened, Father?" Louey asked.

"It seems we've made a mistake." He looked grim but his voice was calm, so we knew it was not something awful.

"What sort of mistake?"

"Well, we were so engrossed in our extremely interesting Conversation about the Oversoul, which we started in the barn when we went to get the seeds, that we didn't pay proper attention to our task."

"Oh dear, sounds like me," Louey said.

"Yes," her father agreed. "Exactly. What I scold you about so much. Now we've discovered that we've sown several different kinds of grain in this one field, and we are not quite sure what crop we'll get."

"Oh, this mistake is bigger than the ones I make," Louey said happily.

"How is that?" her father asked.

"Because it won't disappear. It will just grow and keep growing. You'll all have to watch it every single day."

"And we'll water it and weed it and help it grow." Brother Bronson turned to his Consociates. "We might as well go back to planting and finish the field. Whatever grows will grow. We'll have to leave it to Providence."

The others set off for their work areas.

"Now it's your turn to scold me, daughter, as I scold you when you have been foolish."

"Oh no." Louey giggled. "I think it's wonderful. I'll bet there never was a farm before with a secret crop."

"You're right," he said sadly. "We'll know nothing till we see the plants."

I had never seen the schoolmaster look so glum. Then he spoke softly, as if to himself. "I have put my heart and soul and hopes into Fruitlands—"

"Father," Louey said brightly, taking his hand, "since even the cleverest detective could not solve this now, you have created a great mystery. Ladeez and gentlemen!" She seized a stick and pointed it at the field. "The Consociates are proud to present . . . the Great Fruitlands Mystery!"

She had managed the impossible. She made her father smile. In fact, he laughed.

"Louisa," he said, "you have a marvelously creative mind. And your mother's ability to rescue me from despair. My dear child, you absolutely restore my faith. Join our mystery, the two of you. Help us sow."

With the greatest delight, Louey and I did. Pa had never let me help him sow. Now I scattered unknown seeds and looked forward to the secret crop.

I took note of which corner had my seeds so that I would know which plants were my own private mystery.

Dear Diary,

Hallelujah! Sister Abigail got back her lamp!

Last evening during their Conversation, she just spoke right out. (Today Louey acted it all out for me like a play.)

SISTER ABIGAIL: I must have my lamp back.

BROTHER CHARLES: There will be no lamps here at Fruit-
                       lands that burn animal oil.

SISTER ABIGAIL: Then you will each have to learn to mend your own clothing. I cannot manage by bayberry candle. I shall do no more sewing and mending. None!

(The schoolmaster rushes to her side.)

SCHOOLMASTER: Abba dear, you need your lamp. Your eyesight is poor. You do so much for all of us. Of course you must have it back.

BROTHER CHARLES *(vexed)*: Willy, go fetch her lamp. But remember, there is no cash for more oil once this is burned.

SISTER ABIGAIL: Then I shall write to my brother Sam in Lexington for a loan. I trust I shall have my light from now on whenever I need it. I cannot live without proper light.

(Curtain)

Diary, I am so glad for her! I'm sorry for the whales but I'm gladder for her. Sister Abigail is more important to me than any whale.

Willy plays chess with me almost every day. He is very patient and I have learned all the moves. Today I checked him twice and he said I'm very smart. I know I'm not very smart, Diary, but maybe I am a little smart. That would be enough for me.

When Pa heard about the Fruitlanders mixing seeds in the same field, he laughed himself clear off the rocking chair.

Aunt Nell had to help him up. I never saw him take on so. On Monday he's going to go over and give the neighbors a hand with planting fruit trees and straightening things out.

Monday is going to be a real holiday. Another event is set for then, too. All the Fruitlanders are going to give up their regular everyday dress and put on their special costumes. Brother Charles designed them and Sister Abigail and Anna and Louey and Elizabeth have been sewing them.

I helped, too. I sew pretty good. Aunt Nell taught me basting and hemming, and then Anna showed me some new stitches. Anna is very nice. She's quiet and rather serious. I guess that's 'cause she's the eldest sister, but she's kind.

The clothes are made of linen, a good cloth because it comes from flax, which is a plant. There are brown linen tunics for everyone, trousers of the same stuff for the men and skirts for the women. Broad-brimmed hats keep off the sun. Canvas sandals have replaced leather shoes. Too bad, no tree bark with vine laces and bluebell tassels.

I sure like the way the costume looks, but I know Pa wouldn't care for me to even try it on.

Sister Abigail has made me a sun hat. Surely Pa won't mind that!

He doesn't dislike the Fruitlanders. He just doesn't understand them. And he's kind of scared of them. 'Cause he can't tell what they'll do next.

Aunt Nell is more like me. We don't understand, either, but we aren't scared. We think they're good folk.

10. Pa Shakes My Hand

Pa was carrying his basket of vegetables again, but this morning he didn't just walk on ahead of me. He kept pace right beside me, and, after a while, he actually began to talk to me. First he cleared his throat a few times as if there were several frogs in it—and a tadpole or two.

Finally he spoke. "Say, er, Susan—er—what does that schoolmaster teach best?" Pa almost sounded like he had a stammer.

"Gymnastic spelling," I answered quick, and I then tried to explain and to act out some letters. I crossed my arms for *X* and rounded my back for *C* and walked stiffly for *I*. Without King Alfonso or Lady M's help, I answered my pa straight out.

He watched and listened and didn't say anything else for a while. "Not like my schooling," he observed at last. "No sirree. Those days the schoolmaster had a cane and he'd whup you if you answered wrong. What else do you study there?"

As best I could, I began to describe the lessons to Pa. Though I stammered, I made myself keep going. Once or twice I had to stop and blow the letters out the way Anna had showed me. Pa just heard me out, and when I was through he walked along silent and thoughtful. It was a real talk. I had dreamed about walking along and talking to Pa, but I'd never believed it would happen.

Suddenly Pa stopped dead in his tracks.

The Fruitlanders were all out in front of the farmhouse, dressed in their new outfits.

"We come on the wrong morning," Pa muttered, half turning to run back. "Must be a circus or somethin' special going on."

"No, Pa. That's the Fruitlands outfit. All linen. Remember?"

He nodded. Mercifully, he kept his peace.

My own friends, light and airy as moths, flitted about in the meadow. May looked like a little fairy. But the grown-ups standing around looked passing strange, their floppy, lightweight tan outfits ballooning in the early breeze. Brother Joseph, particularly, his great beard waving above the tunic, looked a sight.

I supposed their new dress'd take some getting used to for Pa—and even for me.

Anna saw us coming. "Doesn't everyone look special?" she greeted us.

I grinned and nodded 'cause it was true.

Then Willy hurried over. "Morning, Susan. Sir." He'd never met Pa before. He bowed. "May Susan come and play a quick game of chess? I'm to help with the planting later, but I've got the board all set up."

"Chess? Eh . . . did you say chess?" Pa seemed confused.

"Yes, P-Pa. Willy's teaching me." I held my breath, hoping Pa was not against chess. He'd never said so. "It's a n-nice game," I added. "There's knights and k-kings and castles—"

"I played chess myself when I was a youngster," he told me.

"Then perhaps you can practice with Susan," Willy suggested. "I think she's going to be a strong player."

Pa looked at me like I was a two-headed calf. I mean, he really really really looked at me. "You don't say. Chess, eh? Well, chess is no game for dummies."

"No sir. May she come and play?"

"Go 'head. I've other business here." Pa carried his basket inside.

A tall, city-dressed stranger came out of the house and stood with the men, who held shovels and picks and rakes and every manner of garden tool needed to plant young trees.

"That's Mr. Emerson, a great poet and a good friend of Father's," Anna whispered. "He's come with another friend—Mr. Thoreau, also a poet—who's inside talking to Marmee. They're here especially to celebrate the planting."

Pa came out again with Sister Abigail, who took him over to the visitor. Mr. Emerson shook hands with Pa and began to speak to him.

Near the chessboard on the green, carefully laid aside, Louey had placed a hat made especially for me. I put it on at once. Its wide floppy brim was a perfect sun umbrella.

We started our game, but there wasn't enough time to think or plan, and Willy beat me easy. Then he showed me some neat moves. Willy was an amazing chess player. His father had taught him; he said his father was a chess master and that was the best you could be.

Meanwhile everyone was joyous, talking and laughing together as if we were all on some glorious summer outing. Fruitlands, that morning, felt like paradise. If life could be like this always, fresh and pleasant in the sunshine, no one having a care, then I would come to believe in the Newness, too.

"Time to plant," the schoolmaster announced.

"Please put these away inside," Willy asked me, handing me the box and board, and he ran to help Brothers Joseph and Everett, who were starting to pack young trees carefully into a cart. Pa was right there, too, working and advising. He knew just about everything there was to know about planting.

"Mr. Thoreau is going to take us on a nature walk through the woods," Louey told me. "That will be our schooling today while the tree planting is going on. Look! Here he comes out of the house."

A young man was walking toward us. He had a large nose and deep-set eyes hidden under heavy, shaggy eyebrows. He wore a most odd-looking, shapeless hat. Louey introduced me and he took my hand and clasped it tight. Though he was not handsome, he was wonderful friendly.

"I'm glad to meet you. Louey's told me all about you." He was the only grown-up who called her Louey. "Since these are your woods, Susan, you shall show the way."

"Oh no, s-s-sir," I said, and felt myself blushing.

"I shall walk close behind you," he insisted, "and study the territory. I'm a surveyor, you know. I make maps. Lead us to your favorite spot. Share it with us."

"A-All right, s-s-sir."

"You are one of a long line of illustrious stammerers," he added. "Did you know that the greatest orator—speaker—in ancient Greece—"

"Where Socrates lived?"

He looked pleased that I knew that. "Yes. The man who made the best speeches there was Demosthenes, who had terrible trouble speaking."

"How c-c-could that be?" I asked.

"He just couldn't say a single word easily, so he made up his mind to conquer it. He did all kinds of exercises. He even practiced talking with pebbles in his mouth."

"Well, m-my pa sure wouldn't stand for that," I said. "He'd c-c-call it a tomfool notion. He'd s-say I might swallow the pebbles and choke on 'em."

"He'd be right. It's a dangerous idea. But Demosthenes defeated the stammer. And so shall you, Susan. Without pebbles."

"I want to go," May begged. "I want to go on the hike."

"You'll get too tired," Sister Abigail said, but May kept insisting.

"Please let her," Elizabeth pleaded.

"Oh, well. She's in her stubborn stage," Sister Abigail said. "Don't make it too long a walk, and she can go."

So we set out, single file, first me, then Mr. Thoreau, then Louey, Elizabeth, and May, and Anna was last.

Soon Mr. Thoreau took out a flute, and as he began to play the sunny woods seemed to hum with music. I don't remember ever in my whole life feeling so free and gay.

Perhaps it was the enchanted Fruitlands hat.

I kept looking back over my shoulder as we walked. I was the leader!

Even though Mr. Thoreau had his eyes cast downward, going over every inch of the ground as we went, he kept on recognizing all sorts of birds. He spotted a squirrel here and a raccoon there, a baby chipmunk peeking out at us and a lovely bird's nest with eggs in it. More as if he sensed than saw the creatures out there and the life in the woods all around us.

We had been walking for about twenty minutes when my own eyes lit on a treasure. How had I passed here a million times before and never noticed it? I picked it up.

"An arrowhead!" I called out to the others. "Perfect!" Not a splinter, not a chip off it, smooth and sharp as if an Indian brave had just shot it from his bow.

"Wonderful!" Mr. Thoreau said, examining it. "If your eyes are sharp, these woods are filled with surprises."

Then everyone began to search the path for treasures. Louey found a spear tip only slightly chipped. Anna and Elizabeth weren't lucky this trip, but little May picked up a heavy jagged rock and insisted it was an arrowhead. "Indians!" she said, her eyes big and filled with awe. She looked around for someone to carry it for her. We all loved May, but this was a heavy rock. "Elizabeth," she asked, "would you carry my Indian rock for me?"

Elizabeth rarely said no to anyone.

"May," Anna said gently, "that is not really an Ind—"

"Please, Anna," Elizabeth interrupted, "I want to do it for her."

"Exchange it for a smaller one," Louey whispered in Elizabeth's ear. "May will never know."

Elizabeth shook her head. Not she. She had a tender heart. And she loved May so, she couldn't bear to fool her. So, of course, she ended up toting that heavy rock no more an Indian arrowhead than Aunt Nell's mortar.

Mr. Thoreau pointed to sweet fern and bright cardinal flowers, to prunella and indigo, to bilberry bushes and sharp-smelling yarrow, to all the various wildflowers and different shrubs as we came upon them. Some, the common ones, I knew. But he showed us new ones, the dwarf andromeda with whitish blossoms, and viburnum.

"You must know where the best berry patches are hiding," he said to me.

"Oh, I do—blackberry and huckleberry and a special secret place where the high bush blueberries grow. And raspberries, too. Which will you have?"

"Huckleberries today," he chose, "for I love them best. Did you know that the Algonquian Indians showed huckleberries to the early settlers and taught them to eat them? Food was mighty hard to come by in the colonies, so huckleberries were a major find. And it was the Indians who gave them to us as a gift."

"But we haven't any baskets with us . . . "

"Lead on, lead on, and the woods will provide the baskets," he promised.

Well, I didn't see how, but I led the way toward the best secret huckleberry patch I knew of, aside a small hidden lake.

When Mr. Thoreau first caught sight of the water, he stopped and smiled. "A lake is like an eye of the earth," he said.

Peeling some lengths of bark from a birch tree, he began to weave the strips into a basket. His fingers were so nimble and swift that right soon each one of us had her own container. May's container even had a strong handle.

"Now we can berry to our hearts' content," he said, stooping suddenly to pick up a lovely red feather. "A scarlet tanager has been by," he noted, tucking the feather into a small compartment sewed into his hat. The hat had tiny pockets for many other small finds.

"What a fine hat!" I said. "Like a cupboard."

"I made it myself." He was proud of it. "It carries my samples and leaves my hands free."

Whenever a bird called, he could tell from the song what bird it was. He knew trees and rocks and moss and mushrooms. It seemed to me he knew everything about the outdoors, and he loved it all.

I loved it, too, but wished I knew more. Pa was dead wrong. I did need more schooling. I didn't know near enough for a girl. Because a girl can't ever know enough.

"How did you learn the names of all the flowers and birds, Mr. Thoreau?" I asked.

"Oh, whenever I spot a new one, I ask folks about it or look it up in books," he said. "It's my favorite occupation."

"I never knew learning about nature could be an occupation." I thought of my folks, who worked most days from sunup to sundown. "How do you have the time for it?"

"Susan, I believe a man should work one day a week and have the other six for his joy and wonder."

I gulped. I was mighty glad Pa was back planting trees and not along to hear that.

When Mr. Thoreau first said it—one day of work and six days of doing what you want—the idea seemed sinful. After I'd considered it, I actually began to agree. What's wrong with doing what you love to do best most of the time? Isn't that a kind of paradise?

Then we finally stepped into the open glade. Right before us were the bushes bending over, heavy with berries, and there were more on a hill nearby. First we had an eating party. We ate and we ate, then we sat resting in the sun while Mr. Thoreau played us some more music.

Then he suggested we fill our baskets with berries to bring back for the others at Fruitlands.

"Let's see who gets the most," he said, and that set us off on a picking race. Each of us wanted to gather the most berries. Little May picked so hard—her lower lip pushed out and her face sweating in the sun—that we all snuck berries into her basket so she'd win.

"How many do you have, May?" someone would ask, and then take the basket and pretend to count while pouring more into it.

"What do you say to a wash-off in the shallow part of the pond?" Mr. Thoreau suggested. "If you think you need it."

"Oh, we need it," Anna said, and we laughed as we noted one another's sticky hands and berry-stained faces and arms and clothes. We were practically purple.

"You can go wading," Mr. Thoreau said, "but take care. The rocks are slippery."

The cool water was lovely. We splashed about, cleaning ourselves off, a perfect way to end the afternoon. Then we started the hike back.

This time Mr. Thoreau led. He said he could probably lead us back blindfolded, but it would take too long. I believed him. Anna took a turn carrying May's rock. I brought up the rear, holding May's hand. We went along steadily, but slowly because we were tired. May and I did our best to keep up.

After a while, we came to a stand of old chestnut trees where I knew there was a secret spring. It welled up at the base of the largest tree. My mouth was very dry. I decided a cool drink would help us both go faster. "May, let's take a drink of the sweetest water in the world," I said. "We'll catch up with the others in a second."

She and I turned just a few steps off the path, and there was the fresh spring with its lovely, still, small pool trapped in the great roots, the water bubbling up fresh then flowing off to one side.

I held May as she bent over and drank, then set her down on some rocks behind me as I kneeled down to drink. I had me a refreshing drink and was lowering my head for a second one when I saw a terrible reflection in the water.

May! Standing behind me on the rocks looking down. And then bending over laughing and reaching with both hands to pick up something. A young copperhead!

Unmistakable: the hazel-colored body with hour-glass markings on top and a pinkish white belly with dark markings.

May had grabbed the snake tight under its head with her left hand while her right hand was pulling at the tip of its tail, extending it up and down in front of her like a ruler. "Pretty rope," she said. "See what I found? See my pretty rope, Susan?" She was smiling proudly.

I knew if I said, "May, throw that away quick," she'd just laugh and want to keep it even more. May loved to tease.

What should I do? *Grab it from her, Susan. Quick!* my mind ordered me. But suppose I tried to grab it from her and she wouldn't give it up? If she didn't let go, she'd be in fearful danger. We'd both be.

"May," I said softly, rising and walking back toward her till I was real close. "May, can I have a turn holding the pretty rope?"

She shook her head.

"I'd like to look at it." I tried to smile.

"No," she said. "It's for Marmee."

"Please, May—"

"For Marmee," she repeated, grinning ever so proud of herself.

"May . . . please. It's so beautiful. Won't you let me have a turn?"

"It's a present for Marmee," she said again, stubbornly, backing away a little.

"I'll give it right back to you. I only want to look at it."

"You can see it later."

"Please, May. It's so unusual. How did you ever find it? I didn't see it, and I'm much older than you."

Well, she was so proud of finding it that finally she thrust it at me to admire.

117

Aunt and Pa had often talked of snakes. Pa was bit once on the ankle when he was hoeing, but luckily it was only a garter snake. I knew to be scared of copperheads. Aunt warned me to be on the lookout whenever I went walking alone. I was careful. I knew a snakebite could kill. Fast.

I stiffened my body straight up tall, making myself into the letter *I*, tried to stop trembling, and grabbed. The second I clutched its scaly body, I raised my hands high as I could and tossed that copperhead as far away from us as was possible.

Of course, May began to howl at once.

I joined right in with her. "Help!" I hollered. "Help! Mr. Thoreau! Louey! Anna! Elizabeth! Come help us!"

Shouts answered instantly. The others came crashing back through the bushes, and then we were surrounded by them.

"Susan threw away my pretty rope!" May wailed. "It was for Marmee. It was a present. Bad Susan! Bad, bad, bad!" She stamped her foot.

"She was holding a copperhead," I explained. "We were drinking at the spring, and she picked it up on the rocks."

Their faces were very grave.

Her crying only got louder. "Susan, give me back my present for Marmee," she begged. "You promised."

I felt bad. All our explaining that it was a snake and not a rope and that it would have hurt her did not comfort her.

"Come, let us find an even better present." Mr. Thoreau took her hand and led her off toward a huge oak tree. "How about we collect a fairy tea set for Marmee?" he suggested. "All of you stay close together and wait," he told us. "Rest yourselves for the walk back. Everything will be just fine."

May was sobbing. Mr. Thoreau began to gather acorns, showing her how the caps make dainty fairy teacups. Near a bird's nest he searched out several delicate light blue eggshell halves left from recent hatchings. He put them in her hand. They made perfect bowls. Then he sat a long time talking to May until, at last, she quieted down. When she was peaceful he left her with her sisters, and he came to talk to me.

"It was my f-f-fault for stopping to d-drink," I wept.

"No." He shook his head. "You were very brave, you did exactly the right thing. You thought quickly and acted wisely. Your folks will be very proud of you."

Louey walked over and promised, "I'm going to write a play about you. It will be a real true-life drama, and you'll be the heroine."

Maybe in Louey's play I'd be the heroine, but I was the villain as far as little May was concerned. She hated me. I was worse poison than any snake. It would take a long while for her to forgive me, if she ever did. She loved her "pretty rope." Even though everyone kept saying over and over it had been a dangerous snake, she didn't believe them. May didn't even know what *dangerous* meant.

We started back. By then, we were really tired, but once Mr. Thoreau began to play his flute, we moved along steadily enough. We carried brimming baskets of berries for Sister Abigail, who was delighted to get them. May gave her the tea set of eggshell bowls and acorn-top cups.

"We shall have a tea party," she promised May.

That night, when I told Pa and Aunt Nell about the copperhead, I saw them look at each other funny—like they had some secret they weren't telling—then Aunt Nell kissed my cheek and said I was the bravest girl in the world.

Pa rose up from this rocker and said, "Let me shake your hand, girl." And he did, pumping it up and down like he was drawing water at the well. Then he sat down again and said "Amen!" to himself several times, even before he began to read his Bible.

They were mistaken. I wasn't brave. All my life I'd been fearful, a coward afraid of high places and darkness—and snakes. Whatever happened at the spring hadn't been up to me. I didn't think clear or even know I was doing it. Brother Bronson would probably say it was the Inner Spirit in me. The goodness coming out and taking over.

Whatever it was it worked miracles. It got Pa to shake my hand.

11. Strangers in Paradise

Pa went and rummaged in the attic. He found the chess set his father, Grandpa Wilson, had carved out of applewood for him. The board was cloth, rolled up and tied with white ribbons; his ma—my grandmother—had woven it for him. It was lovely.

"Did you play, too?" I asked Aunt Nell.

She laughed at the idea. "Girls didn't play chess in my day. I guess they didn't think we were smart enough."

"I'll teach you once I learn," I promised.

Pa said he'd play me when I was ready.

"I could try right now," I said. "I know the rules."

He beat me pretty fast, and he hadn't played in years.

"You got to know the rules and the moves," he said. "You can keep the set out so's you can practice."

In a funny way, paradise next door was spreading on-to our farm. I woke up happy, and I went to bed happy those days.

Visitors were coming all the time now to Fruitlands to see the New Eden. These outsiders were curious about the experiment of living together and sharing. "Does it work?" they asked. Same as I wondered. "Does not thinking about money and not eating meat make people better human beings?"

Ladies with parasols and gentlemen in jackets walked about the fields and the orchard and came and sat in our schoolroom and listened to our lessons. I got to meet them and to hear them discussing all the paradises they'd visited. Because it turned out there were many folks in different places experimenting at living together and being good and pure.

"The dream," the schoolmaster explained, "is to build a utopia."

Till I heard the strangers talking, I'd believed Fruitlands was the only place of its kind. But not too far away, in West Roxbury, was Brook Farm, another utopia much bigger than ours. And even closer to us, on the Nashua River nearby, was a Shaker village, a utopia, where no one was allowed to live with his family. At Fruitlands they were discussing this idea.

"Men live separate from women; children, too, have to live separate instead of with their parents," Louey told me one day when we were putting fresh flowers on Ma's grave. The Rambling Readers had voted to visit the churchyard once a week.

I didn't understand that utopia at all. "I miss having a mother so much," I said, looking at the grave. "If my ma was alive, I wouldn't want to give her up."

"Every Shaker is supposed to care for everyone else, so being a relative doesn't matter," Louey explained.

"It'd matter to me," I insisted. "I'd want to be with my own true kin."

"Me too," Louey said. "Me too! Doubled." The way the Shakers lived scared her.

But not Brother Charles. He admired the Shakers. He visited them and found their farm prosperous. He came back with a new saying: "The universal good is greater than the family good." Whatever that meant. Seeing Sister Abigail get red in the face every time he said it, I confided to Louey, "He's talking against your mother. She's the biggest believer in *family* in Fruitlands. That ain't right."

After revisiting the Shakers, he said proudly, "They regard me as their true friend 'in the world.'"

Why, he talked "Shaker this" and "Shaker that" so much I was surprised that no one lost patience and grabbed him by the shoulders and tried to shake him. One day Sister Abigail had to go see that utopia for herself.

Afterward she said privately, "Their fields and crops are doing well, but they do not look happy. The women, particularly, look daunted and servile, while the men strut about."

Why don't you say something direct to Brother Charles? I wondered. But, of course by now, I knew why. Sister Abigail needed to keep the peace at Fruitlands because her husband loved his dream. Still, it was easy to tell what she thought of the Shaker utopia. Family was everything to Sister Abigail.

The folks who visited all declared how much they admired what the Fruitlanders were trying to do, but few of them stayed for more than one meal; porridge and apples, bread and water, purslane and dandelion green salad didn't satisfy their bellies, I guess.

"Come join us," Brother Charles would offer, but they would go away. Once in a while a stranger believing in the Newness would actually bring his belongings and come to stay. But the ones who joined were rather peculiar. I watched each of them with interest.

Some were Come-Outers, no longer attending church because of the slavery question. When the church wouldn't condemn slavery, they said the church was a hypocrite. Brother Wood and Brother Joseph were Come-Outers, along with Brother Everett. Others of like belief wandered by.

Mr. Larned came. He'd already lived one year on apples and a second year on crackers. He didn't believe in

clothing, Anna confided to me. He loved the sun; whenever he could, he went off by himself to sunbathe. Nude.

"Nude? Without any clothes on at all?" I was shocked.

"He goes far away in the woods, so no one ever sees
him. Father says there's no harm in it," Anna said matter-
of-factly.

I thought it over. Maybe there wasn't any harm in it; I
wasn't sure. I was sure it was best not to say a word about
Mr. Larned's sunbathing to Pa.

One real scorching week, Mr. Larned wandered off
by himself, and he got a terrible sunburn. First he was
pink as a ham and all swoll up, and then he began
to peel like an onion. When his skin stopped coming
off and he wasn't so stiff and could walk around again, he
departed.

Then along came a man who liked to shout out sudden
and loud whenever he felt the spirit. He believed in freedom of expression. So did the Fruitlanders, and they wel-
comed him. Well, it turned out that he most often felt the
spirit in the middle of the night, and his shouting would
wake up the whole household. So he took his free expression elsewhere.

Other recruits came, too. Some stayed awhile, but
most left almost at once, as soon as they'd sampled a single
Fruitlands dinner or spent the night sleeping on a pile of
straw on the floor.

Then Fruitlands lost Brother Everett. That was sad. He had come on the first day of the experiment and stayed all through the difficult times. He never did say much, but he worked endlessly—Louey said harder than a beaver.

He was most considerate. "Let me help," he'd say to Sister Abigail about the bread baking and the wash and the other heavy household chores. He and the schoolmaster were the only two men to help in the house. They didn't care if it was "woman's work."

Everyone on the farm was mighty fond of Brother Everett. Even my pa liked him. "They never should have locked him up for being daft," Pa said. During the tree planting they'd teamed up, and Pa was impressed by his tireless labor. "Most sensible man on the place," Pa had said. "Certainly makes a person wonder. . . . "

"His relatives must be greedy, wicked people who wanted his property," Louey argued. "The same kind of people who declared their old neighbors were witches back in Judge Sewall's days."

Time and again, we children tried to puzzle out why his relatives had put him in an asylum. One day in the meadow we even held a secret vote: Anna, Louey, Elizabeth, me, and Willy. It came out 5 to 0 that we believed there was nothing wrong with Brother Everett, and his kin were the ones who were touched.

"Let's tell him he won unanimously," Louey urged.

127

Anna was against that. "I think it's best not to bring back painful memories," she said, and she won us over.

One day at lunch, Brother Everett came up with the idea of planting turnips. "They're mighty easy to grow and they're good nourishing food," he said.

"No," Brother Charles ruled. "Turnips grow in the ground, in the darkness away from the sun. They are not fit food for Fruitlanders. Our food must grow in the solar light."

I looked around to see who would speak up; they were already growing carrots and potatoes, root crops, and eating them regular.

"Perhaps, Father—" Willy started, but his father stared down at him with such a stern eye, he stopped.

Nobody else spoke up, including me. I understood that Brother Charles might right then decide to cut out carrots and potatoes, too. I thought, in this paradise, Brother Charles has too much power.

Brother Everett must've been thinking along the same lines. Because the next morning he came in and bid everyone good-bye, saying simply, "My light is not yours, Brothers and Sisters. You have aided my spirit, but now I feel I must move on." Then he took out gifts for each of us children, wooden animals he'd whittled.

A lot of carving went into those gifts, so he must have long been planning to leave. Maybe the turnip discussion had firmed up his mind. He was not content at Fruitlands.

He told why each gift was special.

"For May, a little donkey, 'cause of her stubbornness," he said. "For Elizabeth, a lamb for being gentle. Willy gets a monkey with one arm raised, for his swinging from a branch. For Anna, I've made a fawn to mark her gracefulness. Louisa gets a unicorn, an imaginary animal, 'cause she lives in her imagination. And Susan gets a whopping big copperhead."

It was as long as a walking stick.

"It's beautiful," I said, admiring the perfect carving, "but the snake was only a baby copperhead."

"It's this big by now." Brother Everett smiled. "Besides, you were brave, and I want you to remember that."

He'd carved it so cleverly. It had hidden joints so it could wiggle on the ground, but if I held it up it was perfectly straight.

May wanted my copperhead the minute she saw it, but I said, "I'll only give it up if you give me your donkey," and she would never do that.

We knew we'd miss Brother Everett greatly, but he wasn't happy there. Paradise, apparently, wasn't for everyone.

With all this company around, I got so I was talking pretty good and losing my old shyness. "You are flowering, child," Sister Abigail said one afternoon when I was playing chess with Louey. "Your mother would be ever so proud of you." Louey checkmated me, but it didn't matter after those words.

Mr. Emerson came back to visit many times. He admired the Newness very much, but the first time when Mr. Thoreau came to visit with him, I overheard Mr. Emerson say about the Fruitlanders, "In July they look well. I shall have to wait and see them in December."

Paradise didn't look perfect to Mr. Emerson.

Still, it was the best summer of my life. The weeks just sped by. I even got to sleep over at Fruitlands sometimes. The girls slept on straw mattresses set on the floor way up in a tiny dark attic room with a low-sloping ceiling.

Spending the night proved great fun. We talked way into the middle of the night, and Louey told ghost stories, but I wasn't too scared because we were all lying real close together, warm and safe. We girls could scream loud enough to scare away any ghost if we had to. Especially baby May. She had a tiger's scream. Except she slept so sound she'd never see the ghost.

One time when I slept over it rained, and Louey was pleased by the pitter patter of the drops on the tin roof. "Listen. It's such a pretty noise," she said happily.

And it was. I didn't realize rain could sound so lovely. Fruitlands made me look around and listen and think.

In Pa's farmhouse, I had my own room and my own bed, but I'd have taken a mattress on the floor in an attic any time, with friends. Who needed a bed?

One evening I played a game of chess with Pa and, finally, I won! I couldn't believe it. I said I hoped he didn't pretend and make me win.

"Where would you get that idea?" he said, frowning. "I never cheat."

I didn't think letting the other person win was cheating exactly, but I wouldn't argue. I'd won!

Early next morning, I went hurrying with my incredible news to Fruitlands, but when I arrived, Louey was already out on the grass waiting for me, hopping about madly. Standing on one leg, she shaded her eyes with her hand, and, once she caught sight of me, she raced downhill to meet me. I started to run up toward her.

"Surprise! I'm so happy," she called out. "A new member has joined us. A woman!"

Her dearest wish at last. No wonder she'd been hopping about.

"That's grand." I hugged her.

"She'll be a friend to Marmee, and she'll help with the work. Father says the new member just loves the Newness. She says it has changed her life. She will teach us, too."

"What's her name?"

"Sister Ann Page."

"I can't wait to meet her, Louey. I have news, too. I beat Pa at chess last night."

"Hurrah! Let's find Willy and tell him."

I'd never once beat Willy yet. When we told him, he covered his eyes and pretended to shrink back from me with fear. Then he laughed and shook my hand. "Good show!" he said. "Well done!"

Eagerly we hurried in for our lessons. A stout elderly person was waiting for us. First thing she said was, "The Newness has made a new woman of me. The old sinner I was is gone. Dead!" Second, she announced, "Children, I am a poet."

She was a mighty large woman with disheveled gray hair. She kept losing her hairpins left and right. They just popped out of the bun at the back of her head. Aunt Nell never lost a hairpin, so I figured poets must be special.

Then Sister Ann began her real talking. And she went on talking for a very long time about her own poetry, particularly her poem called "The World." The idea—the *inspiration*, she said, letting us know it was meaningful— came to her in a brilliant flash. It was brought on by the wise saying, 'The world is a many-headed monster.' *The world* means 'the multitude.' She paused and waited to see how that hit us. Her pausing and waiting was exactly what our preacher did when he thought he'd said something important. Usually I didn't understand him. Now I didn't understand her.

Here's when Louey got into hot water. First off, she scowled, which only meant that she was thinking. Then she declared very slowly, "I don't see how you can think that about the world. Father says people are all basically good. Look out the window at the sunshine. The meadows and the woods are glowing. And think of the good people all over. The world is such a wonderful place!"

Sister Ann cleared her throat. "You are only a child," she replied coldly. "You are not expected to understand literature."

She couldn't have said a more hurtful thing to Louey.

"Father and Mother both think I understand. I read Plutarch and Byron and Goldsmith and Dickens. I, too, write poetry."

"That is all well and good," Sister Ann said, while her voice told not one bit of it was well and good, as far as she was concerned. "Let us proceed to our lessons."

"I love poetry," Louey continued passionately. She began trying to make amends because she had spoken so hastily and Sister Ann was miffed. "I love all poetry. Truly I do."

But Sister Ann was no longer listening. She addressed herself to the history lesson.

She proved to be a fussy person. And she was so boring. Not unkind. Just very dull. She did go on and on about her new inner voice that made her purer.

Sister Abigail, however, was delighted to have another woman around for company. Some nights the two of them would sit by Sister Abigail's precious lamp and read to each other or talk. Rather, Sister Abigail would sew and Sister Ann would talk.

Oddly, Sister Ann did almost no work in the house. She did not seem to notice Sister Abigail's constant chores. She spent her time thinking and talking about herself and her poetry. "I this and I that. I this and I that," she would go on.

Louey and I privately agreed that Sister Ann, like Brother Charles, was one of those being rather than doing people. Sister Ann settled in, and Anna said we simply had to let her ride her hobbyhorse.

Of all our teachers, the best was Louey's father. As Brother Joseph said to Pa and me at the woodpile, Brother Bronson had the gift. When he had to go away to Boston or elsewhere with Brother Charles to hold Conversations about the Newness and Fruitlands, I missed his teaching.

The best Nature teacher was Mr. Thoreau.

Sister Abigail's vivid stories were a great treat, but she was too busy to be a regular teacher.

Next, I guess I have to list Brother Charles, whose violin playing was lovely but who kept asking us big unanswerable questions. His latest question was "What is man?" He asked it of us one afternoon.

"A human being?" Anna said.

"A soul and a mind?" Willy guessed.

"A creature who thinks?" I tried.

"An animal with a soul?" Elizabeth wondered.

This Conversation continued for hours. I grew tired of it and nodded off, but Louey pinched my arm and woke me.

Last among our teachers, I put Sister Ann. Even so, I was always polite to her, and I tried to be well behaved. She was striving so hard to be better. One reason I put her last is that I stammered more during her lessons than at any other time. She made me yearn to be out of the schoolroom. I had never felt that way before. But her company made Sister Abigail happy, and I was glad of that because Sister Abigail was so caring and motherly; she treated me like one of her own daughters.

So I was really sorry for my part in what happened next. Sorrier than I could ever say.

Sister Ann started it all one morning. "Susan," she said, "I hear that you have a nice aunt and a father who is a talented gardener. Oh, how I long to meet them."

"I'll tell them," I promised.

Pa just raised his eyebrows when he heard, but Aunt Nell took a fancy to the idea of inviting the new Fruitlander to supper on Friday night next. Aunt was tickled that Sister Abigail had a woman companion in the house for company.

"I accept with pleasure," Sister Ann bubbled. "Why, how hospitable you country folks are. I will come and share my thoughts on the Newness with your family, Susan."

Uh-oh, I thought. Better not try with Pa. Aunt Nell might hear you out, but Pa doesn't believe much in women thinking—about anything.

As for the Newness, it was clear how he felt about that. That very morning he muttered as I was setting out for Fruitlands, "Far as I'm concerned, I prefer the Oldness any day."

Aunt shushed him. "Little pitchers . . . " she warned.

Yes, it would be best for Sister Ann not to share her thoughts with Pa. But she wouldn't look kindly on a child telling her that.

I kept my advice to myself.

12. A Fried Fish Hooks a Poet

Aunt Nell really put herself out. She planned a feast, a vegetarian feast.

She busied herself from real early Friday morning, cooking honey-glazed parsnips, runner beans, stuffed butternut squash, and scalloped sweet potatoes. For dessert she was going to bake a rhubarb pie.

And she had one extra chore because of Pa. He'd been grumbling about a whole evening meal with just vegetables, and how, after a heavy day's work a man needed fish or some other meat on his table.

At breakfast time he appeared in his waders carrying his straw basket heavy with fish. He'd made it his business, first thing on getting up, to go down to the pond, and he'd been lucky.

So Aunt Nell fried up three good-sized perfectly crisp perch.

Before lessons, for this special occasion, I picked a large bouquet of wildflowers for Aunt Nell to set in the center of the table. The flowers looked right nice in the milk-glass pitcher.

Late that afternoon, Sister Ann walked back alongside me. She stopped every few steps and wiped her brow. "You're sure there's no shortcut, child?"

"No ma'am. This is the shortcut."

"This is the longest walk I've had in years," she gasped.

"I thought poets walked a lot," I said. "Mr. Thoreau is a poet, and he hikes."

"Hmm." Sister Ann's face was not enthusiastic about that news.

When I introduced Sister Ann to Pa and Aunt Nell, she was still huffing and puffing from the walk, breathing like we'd climbed Mount Wachusett. Then she settled into Pa's rocker.

"I don't suppose Susan's told you about my poem, 'The World,' which was inspired by the great thought, 'The world is a many-headed monster,'" she began.

"No," Aunt Nell said politely, to show she was listening, as she put the finishing touches on the food. "Do tell." Saying that was a bad mistake.

"Sir Philip Sidney and William Shakespeare were both enamored of the thought of the monstrous multitude," our guest went on.

"You don't say." Pa peered out the window. "I'd best get the grain in soon," he speculated. "We're past due for a storm."

Two of Sister Ann's hairpins escaped onto our kitchen floor. I chased them down and she stuck them back in her bun every which way. Those hairpins did not like her.

Then we sat down and Pa said grace.

Aunt Nell began to bring round the food, first the parsnips then the squash then the beans and, last, the potatoes. Usually, Pa served himself first, but this evening each platter went to Sister Ann first.

The poet helped herself to real big helpings.

Well, I thought, watching, it's mighty lucky that Aunt always cooks a heap of everything so there'll be leftovers, because we're gonna need them this night.

Giant first helpings. Hungry poets were passing strange.

Then Aunt Nell brought round her pretty rose-patterned conserve dishes filled with watermelon pickle and cranberry-apple compote.

After Sister Ann had her turn, the food got passed to the rest of us.

The fish platter, however, went first to Pa, who shoveled the biggest fish onto his plate; then he handed the perch over to me. I took the smallest one, leaving a nice plump one for my aunt.

Out of politeness for our guest, Aunt Nell didn't take any fish, either. Just to keep Sister Ann vegetarian company I guess, which was nice of Aunt Nell because she surely favored perch.

Well, Sister Ann began scooping up vegetables and watermelon pickle and cranberry-apple compote and chewing and chewing, and all the while she was staring goggle-eyed at the remaining perch on the serving dish lying in the middle of that table. It stared right back at her.

Eating didn't stop her none from talking about that one poem of hers. That poem was the many-headed monster. It wouldn't go away.

Pa and Aunt Nell just sat quiet and heard her out. Once in a while there was the ping of a hairpin popping.

Sister Ann's eyes stayed fastened like they were hooked onto that crisped perch. After a while, my aunt couldn't help noticing her guest's fixed gaze. "Would you like to just taste the perch?" Aunt Nell inquired. "I didn't offer you any because—"

"No, no. Of course you didn't. You were right. Quite right, my dear."

"I can't see as how eating this fresh perch right out of the pond is going to ruin your character," Pa said, cutting himself a real big chunk from the fish on his plate. He lifted it up on his fork, but before he put it in his mouth he paused to examine it all around. "It ain't harmed my character one bit and I eat it regular."

"Now, Henry . . . " Aunt Nell chided.

Sister Ann laughed nervously. "I must admit, this is one time when I almost agree with you, Mr. Wilson."

"Well then, just you have some. Nell is one fine cook. You won't get fish like this soon again. Crisp and brown on the outside but just as soft as butter and mighty juicy inside. Why, I don't know when I've had a fish as good as this. Nell, you went and outdid yourself. Too bad Sister Ann won't even taste it."

Sister Ann blushed. "I really oughtn't," she said, "but maybe . . . maybe I will. Just a taste of the tail will do. Just a bit. A teeny teeny bit."

With her thumb and her forefinger crooked round, Sister Ann signaled about an inch of fish was all she'd have.

Aunt Nell picked up the fish platter and carried it round and set it down in front of her. "You just go right ahead and help yourself to whatever you feel like, Miss Page," Aunt Nell said.

Well, she did.

To begin with, she first took the inch she'd said she wanted right off the tail.

I never saw anybody chew food with so much pleasure. And when she swallowed, her whole big body shuddered with the joy of it, sending another hairpin skipping clear across our hearth. Then it was just as if Sister Ann couldn't stop herself.

So we wouldn't watch her knife and fork working on the fish, she started babbling about her poem again. "Yes, the many-headed monster idea can be found in *Coriolanus*—" She swallowed a big mouthful.

"Coria-who?" Pa asked.

"One of Shakespeare's tragedies: *Coriolanus*."

"Can't be one of his good ones. I heard of *Hamlet* and *Macbeth*, but I ain't never heard of this one."

"Sir Walter Scott used the phrase as well"—she took a huge forkful of fish—"and Pope." She giggled. "So I am in excellent literary company."

I tried hard to pull my eyes off the eater, but they just wouldn't go. I knew it wasn't polite for me to stare. But she was eating so much.

Now she'd got Pa's dander up. "The Pope don't impress me," he said shortly.

"Not *the* Pope," she corrected him, using that same cold tone she'd used on Louey. "Alexander Pope, the poet. Oh dear—" She'd spilled some honeyed parsnip sauce into her lap.

Aunt Nell hurried with a clean dishcloth to help her wipe off.

The cleanup took time away from her eating. It made her stop talking about her poem. We had a minute of no talking altogether.

Pretty soon the fish's skeleton was about all that was left—how could I help noticing? Poor Sister Ann must have been starving for fish. Made me wonder, what will she do? Will she go back to Fruitlands and tell them what she ate in our house? And if she does, what will they say?

Aunt Nell had said that very first day that the Fruitlanders left things up to each person's own conscience. Maybe that had been their idea at first. But it wasn't quite the way things were working out. Because the schoolmaster had been troubled by Brother Joseph's milk drinking—even though he only drank it privately.

But Sister Ann was so full of the Newness. How could she go back and tell them she ate a whole crisped perch? Surely a lady who was purifying herself—who was brave enough to write a poem about the world being a many-headed monster—would also be brave enough to tell the truth. And I was almost admiring her for it, in my head. I already liked her better for her honesty.

Well, after her many "thank you's" and "good-bye's," Sister Ann and I started walking back to Fruitlands. Once we were a good way from the house, she stopped and giggled, then said, "Let's keep that little fish a secret between us, shall we, Susan? No one need know."

I halted right there and looked straight up at her. "You askin' me to lie to my fr-fr-friends, ma'am?" I was very upset. And disappointed in her. How could she?

Before she got a chance to answer, a voice hailed us from up the path. Brother Charles, out for an evening stroll. Or maybe he'd been waiting there to accompany Sister Ann? That was thoughtful; then I wouldn't have to walk her all the way home.

"Well, well," he said, "Sister Ann. How did you fare at Neighbor Wilson's house?"

She blinked hard. "Oh, very well. They are kind and generous people. They were extremely interested in my poem."

"Ah! They are good folk. Susan, you must tell me what your aunt Nell's grand menu was this evening. With your pa's abundant garden, you probably had delicious vegetarian treats." Brother Charles's piercing eyes were fixed on my face.

"Honey-glazed parsnips, stuffed butternut squash, runner beans, and sweet potatoes," I mumbled.

"Quite a feast. Was that all?"

"Cranberry-apple compote and watermelon pickle."

He was still waiting.

"And rhubarb pie."

"Has your father turned vegetarian like us?"

I looked at Sister Ann, whose face was a raspberry color now. She was looking straight at me, too. Looking hard.

144

"No sir."

He was waiting.

"Aunt served fish—crisped perch, too."

He threw his head back as if he were swallowing.

"Ah," he said. "Indeed a feast. But I am positive that Sister Ann did not touch the fish. She is a principled person."

I was miserable.

"You must a-a-ask her, s-sir." I waited for her to speak.

Now Brother Charles was gazing at her, too.

"I only tasted the very littlest bit of the tail," she whispered unhappily.

He turned to me, but even though she had not told the truth, I was not going to say one word more.

"I am shocked," Brother Charles told her coldly. "It does not matter how much of the fish you ate. You might as well have eaten the whole thing, for the poor creature had to suffer and die so that you could feed your gross appetite. I would not have believed it. A poet. A woman of sensibility. The author of that grand poem 'The World.' How could you?"

Holding my ears, I turned away. I left the two of them there on the path: he, pale and furious, scolding; and Sister Ann, flushed with embarrassment, hiding her head.

Even though I didn't like her, I felt sorry, ever so sorry, for her. I walked back home real slow, thinking sad thoughts.

Poor poor Sister Ann! She talked so much about the Newness, but it had not really worked for her.

"You're back mighty quick," Aunt Nell said. "Everything all right?"

I nodded. It wasn't, but I didn't want to explain.

"That was one hungry lady," Pa said. "They must be starving her next door. For a vegetarian, she did a right good job on the fish. She ate it like a shark."

"Now Henry," Aunt Nell reproved him, "don't be talking about our guest."

I was heartsick. But of course, I didn't say a word to them about what happened on the path. It was Sister Ann's secret, after all.

Dear Diary,

Sister Ann is gone from Fruitlands. I know some of the blame is mine—even though Louey heard me out about the fish and says not so. It seems that after Brother Charles walked back with Sister Ann, he announced in the common room that she had eaten fish.

At that, Sister Ann rushed right out of the room, hairpins popping all over the place. Sister Abigail tried to follow her, but she'd locked her door and wouldn't come out.

Next morning real early, before other folks were even stirring, she was gone. She'd walked to the village and left her packed trunk to follow. On top of the trunk was a note. It said, "This is not a place where poetry can flourish."

A Fried Fish Hooks a Poet

"*I'm real sorry,*" *I told Louey.* "*I didn't mean to get the poet in a pickle.*"

"*You didn't,*" *Louey said.* "*She did it all by herself.*"

"*Still. She was the only woman Consociate. Your mother will miss her.*"

"*Yes, she will. Marmee is disappointed in Sister Ann, but she's furious with Brother Charles for shaming another human being.*"

I told Louey I don't believe the Newness works for some folks, no matter how many apples they eat and how much fresh water they drink. Even when they're trying their best, the little spirit inside them seems not to be good.

Louey looked so sad.

"*I know,*" *she said.* "*The trouble is, Father still believes in it. And as long as he keeps his faith, Marmee says we must support him, for we love him. That is what love is.*"

We were both feeling sort of hopeless when Willy came along.

"*Chess, anyone?*" *he asked. We both shook our heads, but we could see that Willy was sad, too. I think he was ashamed of his pa. Willy is so nice, we couldn't hold his father's actions against him. So both Louey and I said yes together, and we all laughed.*

"*You two can be partners against me,*" *Willy offered.*

"*Yankees against the Redcoats,*" *Louey declared fiercely.* "*No taxation without representation!*"

Willy smiled at her foolery and set up the game. We part-
ners played so hard, Diary, that we plumb forgot all about
poor Sister Ann. Not until I began to write down the day's
events here did I remember her.

Because, guess who won? Yep. The Rambling Readers
won, and we danced around and celebrated something awful.
Last thing Louey said to Willy—to show him we were all
good friends—was, "We must all hang together, Willy, or
we'll all hang separately." Willy clutched at his throat and
staggered off. I think he was glad we'd won.

But how could I forget Sister Ann's trouble so fast? My
Inner Spirit is not very strong, I guess, so I shouldn't be judg-
ing other folks. I'll have to work on being better.

I've won two chess games now, one against Pa and one
partners with Louey against Willy. It is so exciting to be a
winner! It takes your mind off everything and makes it easier
to be a sinner.

Rhyming is fun. Maybe someday I'll write a real poem.

13. Bringing in the Sheaves

"I feel like there's starch in my bones," Aunt Nell grumbled one morning. "My rheumatism is acting up something fearful."

Pa was just sitting down to his bacon and eggs. "Sorry, Nell," he said. "Be sure to take your tonic." Then he began to gallop through his eating. "That's a sure sign"—he took a quick swallow of hot tea that caused him a coughing fit—"there's a storm a-coming in. I smelt it in the wind. And your bones are more reliable than *The Farmer's Almanac*."

Daily he'd been out in the fields from morning till night, tending his crop. He looked forward to a plentiful harvest. Autumn had begun with a long warm spell, and he was anxious to get his grain in before the weather changed.

At Fruitlands, where I was spending most of my time, the harvest looked promising, too. While the Fruitlands mystery field turned out peculiar, my corner was barley and some of the rest was harvestable. The other crops came up strong, and in the bright clear weather the men cut the grain and stacked it in shocks in the fields. For the first time, the place looked like a working farm.

Sister Abigail was the happiest I'd seen her, gazing out her kitchen window at the golden wheat just waiting to be carried in. "There will be bread aplenty all winter," she said several times, and I even heard her humming "Bringing in the Sheaves" as she cooked.

Her happiness was contagious. Louey was very sensitive to her ma's moods, and she caught this one and spread it around, making jokes and playing pranks and teasing.

So with all Pa's harvest hustling at home, I was mighty surprised when I arrived for lessons to see Brother Charles and Brother Bronson standing on the front lawn, dressed up real neat for traveling.

Louey came a-running to meet me. "I have good news and bad news. Choose. Which first?"

"Good."

"I finished writing your play, *Susan and the Copperhead*. Stay and we'll read it after lunch."

My play! I was a character in a play, just like Lady Macbeth. "Oh, Louey!" I was so thrilled, I couldn't say more.

"Now the bad," she said. "Father and Brother Charles are leaving for Boston to hold Conversations on the Consociate life and vegetarianism."

"That can't be," I gasped. One thing I knew for sure was that no farmer ever goes traveling at harvest time. The same way no captain ever deserts his ship.

Before I could ask, "How come?" she told me. "They heard the call of their Inner Spirits and were moved to go."

"Their Inner Spirits must be left over from the city. What about the crop?"

"They say it will keep till they return."

Just then Sister Abigail came down the steps. There was no happy expression on her face, and she sure wasn't humming. Her eyes were downcast and her lips were pursed.

"Brother Charles and I will be away several days, my dear," her husband said, "spreading the light. Do not concern yourself about us."

"But the grain . . . ," she reminded him. "The crop is ripe for harvest."

"Sister Abigail." Brother Charles put his hand out flat in front of him. That always meant *I know better, so stop talking.* "Leave that to us. The grain will wait."

I never should have said a word, but it was as if I needed a cork to stop my mouth. "My pa says a storm is past due. He's hustling to get his barley in this morning."

Brother Bronson frowned with concern at my words.

But his Consociate just smiled. "On what scientific principle did Neighbor Wilson determine the elements?"

"He feels it a-coming. He smelt it in the wind, and Aunt Nell's rheumatism is hurting real bad."

Once again, Brother Charles's mouth cut his face in that stingy smile, and he tapped me on the head like I was a good little puppy and what my pa thought meant nothing at all.

"There are clouds in the east," Sister Abigail noted.

"It will blow over," Brother Charles assured her.

"If it really does look like rain, Abba," Brother Bronson said, "the grain must be saved. Send the children for the other men. They will leave their tasks and bring it in."

He and his companion set out.

Anna, as the oldest among us, was substitute schoolmistress this day. First she read to us about King Arthur and Queen Guinevere and the knights of the Round Table. "They used a round table for fellowship," Anna explained, "so that no one would be at the head. They'd all be equal."

"Like at Fruitlands," I guessed.

"Yes," Anna said. "You're right."

Then we drew pictures of knights and ladies. Willy drew a marvelous castle with a moat all around. I think a moat is a great idea; on hot days you could just step out your door and have a swimming hole.

The morning passed pleasantly enough, though it was hard for me to pay attention. My mind kept wandering to *Susan and the Copperhead*. Louey hadn't even let me have a peek at it while she was writing, though I was bursting with curiosity. She said it was more a melodrama than a play. A melodrama is a story with a lot of heavy action and exaggeration. It's my favorite kind.

I could hardly stay in my seat.

We did our sums, then finished up with mental subtraction. My problem was: "If a pond has 372 frogs living in it and a snake eats 38, how many frogs are left?"

I knew the answer was 334, but I called out, "None, 'cause they all hopped away out of fear."

Everyone liked my answer. Then, of course, I corrected it.

Anna smiled; she might be a schoolmistress one day. She teaches nice.

Oddly, there weren't any grown-ups at lunch other than Sister Abigail. So she sat down with us, which was a treat. Lunch was baked potatoes, salad, apples, and water.

I was looking forward so to the play, I hardly paid attention to what I ate. It didn't matter.

Afterward, back in the empty schoolroom, Louey sat up on the tall chair and little May and I sat regular, and Louey read us the whole play through.

I loved it, every word.

Susan and the Copperhead was eight pages long, and mine was the grandest part in it. The only other characters were May and the talking snake, so I got to say many lines.

Louey bamboozled May into doing her part by promising her that she could hold the copperhead Brother Everett had whittled for me.

Louey (offstage) was going to play the snake's voice. During the reading, she practiced hissing something fearful.

We three slipped off to the barn to rehearse.

Susan and the Copperhead

Opening Scene: *Pile of rocks with a sign* SNAKE *and an arrow pointing upward. The snake is lying on top of the rocks and nobody is in sight. The snake begins its soliloquy. That means it is thinking out loud.*

SNAKE: Heh, heh, heh! Here I lie in wait for a victim. I've dined on 52 worms and 78 bugs and 104 frogs today, but my fangs ache for the taste of a human. With or without a little salt and pepper.

Gadzooks, but I am a hungry viper!

I *must* have a *human* to bite or my teeth will rot. I will lose my reputation as number one vicious viper around here.

(Footsteps and two girls' voices are heard offstage.)

SNAKE: Harken! Lovely girlish voices. Right this way, my proud beauties, and I'll soon have you in my jaws. Heh, heh, heh!

What's this? Children? Oh dear. Well . . . the three-year-old will make a delicious delicacy with dandelion greens. I will lie still as a rope and fool them.

(Loud, long, scary hiss that sounds like a waterfall.)

(Susan enters, with May slightly behind her, happily picking flowers here and there.)

Bringing in the Sheaves

SUSAN: It's been a lovely walk. I have this perfect arrowhead I found, and we all have baskets of berries. (*Puts her hand to her brow.*) But I feel so hot and thirsty! Alas, my throat is parched, and I'm soaked in sweat. I would give my fortune for a fresh cool drink of water.

(*She cups her ear with her hand.*)

Wait! I think I hear splashing.

(*She looks around. Her eyes light upon a washtub of water marked MOUNTAIN STREAM.*)

What luck! We've come upon a freshwater spring. Come along, May. Let us drink some of this lovely cool water.

(*May skips and catches up with Susan, and Susan holds her while she bends to drink. Then Susan sets May down safely on rocks behind, while she kneels to drink.*)

SUSAN: I am so thirsty, I shall drink it all up.

(*She stares into the water and then turns to the audience, shocked.*)

Horrors! I cannot believe what I see!

Just then—as we were getting to the best part—Sister Abigail interrupted our rehearsal. "There's a storm blowing this way fast, children," she said. "I need you to run out and find Brother Joseph and Brother Wood. They must bring in the grain. Louisa, you look in the orchard, and Susan, try the vegetable garden. Willy, Anna, and Elizabeth are already searching elsewhere."

We ran and shouted but we could not find anyone. Nor could the others.

The sky was darkening quickly, and the wind had picked up.

"Marmee, the men were talking last night about a Come-Outers meeting in the village this morning," Louey said. "Maybe they went and are still there."

Sister Abigail tapped her forefinger against her chin. "That would explain why they weren't at lunch," she said. "Then we shall have to bring in the grain ourselves." She looked up at the threatening sky.

"You older children, grab some baskets and pile the wheat in them. May and I will get some old sheets and rope. We'll make bundles and then just drag them along the ground into the barn. Quick, now!"

The golden sheaves were just standing there, leaning on each other and waiting for us. We went right to work.

The wind began to push hard against our bodies.

"Listen to the thunder, Susan," Louey called out in delight as she lugged sheaves to the basket. "It's like an ogre roaring at us to scare us so that he can steal our food."

"Well, he won't get it!" Willy declared fiercely.

Sister Abigail and May came hurrying back with the old bedsheets and ropes. We gathered the sheaves into loose bundles and then we harnessed ourselves in teams of two in order to drag our loads into the barn.

"Susan, are you strong enough to do this?" Sister Abigail asked me as Louey and I started on our first trip.

"Oh yes," I said. "I'm fine. I love doing it."

Back and forth we went, ignoring the wind and the sky's rumbling. Then lightning began to crackle all about us.

Willy, teamed with Sister Abigail, raised his fist high above his head and called out to the heavens. "We shall not be vanquished! *Excelsior!*"

"That's the spirit, Willy," Louey said. "Oh fearful fiend, who comes to steal our winter food, *begone!* There is nothing for you here at Fruitlands."

To be part of the fun as we pulled, I whinnied like a horse.

"Good old Dobbin! You shall have a carrot tonight," Louey promised me. I whinnied again and stamped my foot.

By the time the storm hit in full force, the crop was safe and dry in the barn. Sprawling on the hay, resting, all of us watched the teeming rain.

"Wasn't that exciting, Susan? Wasn't that fun?" Louey asked. "Marmee, we're heroes. When Father knows what we did, he'll be so proud."

"Yes, he will," Sister Abigail agreed. "Proud and grateful to you all. You are truly Consociates."

"We should celebrate," Elizabeth declared.

Sister Abigail smiled. "Yes, children," she said. "Because you saved the crop, I shall make an apple-currant pudding with my last currants. I was saving them for such a special occasion"—she paused—"and perhaps we can go to the theater afterwards?" First she looked at Louey and then at May and me. "That is, if the drama can be readied in time. You have the rest of this rainy afternoon to work on it."

Since we'd lived the story of the play, we all pretty much knew our parts in it. So we answered loud in one voice and one word, "Yes!" And that evening, there was theater at Fruitlands.

After the apple-currant pudding, Willy, Sister Abigail, Anna, and Elizabeth came into the barn. All the ladies wore shawls as if this were an evening out in town. Each of them carried a candle carefully fixed in a lamp glass; Sister Abigail brought her precious oil lamp and supervised the safe stationing of the lights. Flame in a barn is perilous.

With the snake in place, high up so that the audience could see its head sticking out over the rocks, we were about to start when there was a heavy knocking at the barn door. The two Come-Outers had returned. Finding no one in the house, they'd headed over to the barn. They were rain-soaked and worried that we'd lost the crop.

Once they saw the stacks and heard how we'd managed to save everything, they were the two happiest men in Massachusetts. Even Brother Wood was grinning. Grinning!

"If you can hold off a mite," Brother Joseph proposed, "while we dry off and get a bite to eat, we'd like to come to the the-ayter, too."

Of course we held off, and soon they joined the spectators.

The best part of the play was the fearsome ending. In the flickering light surrounded by the vast darkness of the barn stood smiling, innocent, little May holding the dreadful creature stretched straight up before her.

Suddenly everything depended on me.

Life or death. I had to act quickly.

Louey had written my part so brave, I believed in it while I was acting. And I never stammered once.

SUSAN: Please, May, let me see what you've found.

MAY: No. It's a present for Marmee.

SUSAN: *(Voice trembling.)* I've never seen such a lovely rope. How did you ever find it?

MAY: I'm already three. I'm smart.

SUSAN: I'll say you are. And you're very grown up, too. Let me hold your pretty rope. Please.

MAY: No. It's not for you, Susan. I'll find another one and give it to you.

SUSAN: Let me just hold this rope and look at it. As a special favor because it's so unusual. Please.

MAY: *(Grins.)* Well. Oh, all right. Maybe for one minute.

(Bravely, Susan takes the snake at each end and quickly tosses it far onto the green blanket labeled MEADOW piled on the hay.)
MAY: *(Wailing.)* You lost my—
(She is interrupted by a terrible hissing sound.)
MAY: *(Frightened.)* Susan, a rope can't hiss, can it?
SUSAN: It wasn't a rope, May. It was a deadly poisonous snake.
(Susan and May rush into each other's arms and embrace as the evil voice of the snake is heard thundering.)
SNAKE: Curses! Foiled again.

The audience applauded till their hands must've hurt.

We actresses—Louey holding the snake up in front of her—curtseyed and curtseyed some more. May got a turn to hold the snake and curtsey solo. She got the most applause.

Sister Abigail had brought popcorn for a treat, so we sat around chewing it blissfully. And then we went to bed and listened to the music of the rain on the roof.

I prayed to God that night to thank Him for my friends and all the joy they'd brought into my life. I thanked Him specially for my play and asked Him to let things go on like this forever and ever. But, in my heart, I was worried.

14. Flying

"Can't let those folks starve," Pa would say every couple of weeks as he walked over to Fruitlands with a basketload of provisions: potatoes and greens out of the garden, fruits from our orchard and herbs from Aunt's special patch.

"You are too generous. You bring far too much," Sister Abigail protested each time, but Pa always pooh-poohed that.

"My girl practically lives over here," he said. "We've never seen her so happy and healthy. And she's talking so much better. Your husband untied her tongue. Why, I couldn't overpay you no matter how much I carried over."

I knew she was very grateful—because she was terribly worried about the coming winter.

The Consociates needed money. Their barter idea wasn't working. "You can only barter when you have something of value to trade for what you need," Anna explained to me. They had nothing but their good ideas.

Since Fruitlands was not yet producing anything that was valuable for trading, they couldn't buy the few things they needed, like dried beans and peas, lentils, hominy, dried fruits, lamp oil, kitchenware, linen, or even a comb.

The good weather broke after that fearful rainstorm, and we had an early spell of cold. Brother Bronson and Brother Charles began to go away more often. They were looking for recruits for Fruitlands, and they needed to earn some money. Sometimes when they held a public Conversation, people paid to come and listen.

Once they went off on a long trip. When they returned a week later, they had a story to tell. They had walked for a long time, then they'd had to take a ferry.

"When it came time to collect the fares," Brother Bronson said, "Charles and I simply began to explain what we believe. We told them all that money is the root of all evil, and we have renounced it. We explained that we lived together here with our fellow beings in harmony, sharing and striving for peace and goodwill."

Then Brother Charles took up the tale. "The crew and the other passengers as well were exceedingly interested. They asked many questions about vegetarianism and the Consociate life and the Newness. We conversed for the whole journey."

Brother Bronson went on, his eyes bright. "The captain himself decided to take up a collection for us in his hat."

Sister Abigail smiled, pleased that there would be some cash at last for oil for her lamp and kitchen supplies.

"I think every person aboard must have contributed generously, because suddenly we were confronted with a goodly sum."

"And then?" Louey broke in, excited by the adventure.

"And then, my child," Brother Charles answered loftily, "of course, we refused it."

"Refused?" Louey seemed confused.

"Of course, dear Louisa," her father said. "We could not take their money after stating our principles."

"But the whole reason you went, Father—"

"Yes, we do need money," he agreed sweetly, "but we could not garner it in an unconscionable way. We could not go against the Inner Spirit."

There were tears in Louey's eyes. She knew how much her mother was counting on the money. We had worked fearfully hard; we had brought in the grain and saved the crop; we had done all we could. Need had driven us. There wasn't time to consult the Inner Spirit. The Inner Spirit had nothing to do with it.

Sister Abigail's disappointment was plain to see.

"We visited with the Shakers," Brother Charles said. "They continue to prosper and they live in peace. We might learn much from them."

"What might we learn?" Sister Abigail said, annoyed.

"A kind of unselfishness. They recognize that there is individual family good, but then there is the larger universal good—community good."

"Are you saying that to want to be married and have a family of one's own is selfish?" she challenged him.

"Abba, my dear," her husband said, "all Charles is telling you is that the Shakers feel that marriage is a stumbling block to the true life."

"Let me explain," his Consociate said. "Marriage and children do not generate selfishness, but selfishness generates them."

"The Shakers feel a man's wife and family interfere with his spiritual development," the schoolmaster added.

"And how do you feel?" Sister Abigail asked her husband directly. She was very pale.

"Well, a single unattached person is brother to all. So, philosophically their argument has merit. But I do not know how I feel, Abba. I am confused, and I am pondering the problem."

While he pondered, the cold weeks of autumn passed. We continued to have our daily lessons at Fruitlands, but there was no great happiness there.

One bitter afternoon, Brother Wood slipped away for good, departing as silently as he had lived among us. I hope he found a new place with kind people who let him keep his name backward the way he liked it. Wood Abram. I came to like it that way myself. Wilson Susan wouldn't sound near as good. But he had a nice combination.

With blizzards coming, with no new recruits and little money, there wasn't much reason to be cheerful. Mornings as I was about to set out from home, Pa would shake his head and say, "They still there? They'll never make it through the winter."

"Please, Pa, don't say that," I begged.

"It's the truth. They're dreamers, girl. They don't live in the real world."

"Your pa is right, Susan," Aunt Nell said. "You'd best make your mind ready for it."

I couldn't. I just couldn't. They had come and changed my life, and I didn't want them to go.

Pa crammed his basket even fuller with provisions and gave me sacks of food to carry along as well. He was sad, too; he'd become fond of the Fruitlanders, though they were odd. Couldn't get him to admit it, but it was so.

A single delightful celebration broke into the dreary autumn gloom. A double birthday. November 29, 1843, was Louey's eleventh birthday and her father's forty-fourth.

The first snow had fallen the night before—Mother Nature's gift to Louey. That birthday morning we threw

snowballs and tied barrel stays on to our feet for run-
ners; we slid about gloriously for hours. We took a lot of
tumbles as the sun sparkled on the snow, turning it crystal.

"I wish Sister Ann could see this day," Louey said.
"It's so beautiful. Even she wouldn't think the world was
a many-headed monster today."

"I'm not so sure," I said. "She wants to think that. But
I'm glad she's not here talking about that poem of hers."

We built two snow figures, a big one of the schoolmaster with a twig for a nose, and a small one of Louey with a
chestnut nose.

Then May spotted her favorite swinging branch, leaf-
less now but sturdy and tempting. "I want to fly," she
begged, and soon she was dangling happily. The others
began to clamber about on the bare tree, jumping off into
the snow or moving onto a branch to swing.

I watched wistfully. Then once and for all I made up
my mind. *Begone, vile cowardice!* I commanded silently. I
blew away my fear with one powerful puff.

So I was ready, a little later on, when Louey teased me
with her usual invitation to try flying. I surprised her with
a yes.

Only it came out "Y-Y-Yes."

She was delighted. "I'll tell you what. For the first try,
you needn't climb. I'll bring the branch down and Willy
will hold it, so you can grab on. Come on!"

"Louisa," Anna cautioned, "you'd better not—"

"It'll be easy." My friend didn't heed her. "Nothing to it. And the wind will carry you right along, light as a bird . . . "

I would be gliding through the air, flying with the eagles. Well, maybe with the sparrows.

I ran forward as Louey went back up the tree. Willy stood to the side, waiting, and reached up as the bough bent forward under her weight. He caught on and held it. Then the two of them hung on together till I was in the center, grasping it tightly.

When they let go, it sprang up violently, and in a second I was dangling way up in the air, higher than I'd thought possible, the sunlit icy fields rippling beneath me in waves, unbelievably bright and white and distant. It was dizzying.

I shut my eyes.

"Slide your hands along toward the end of the branch. Then push your feet with all your might and swing," Louey shouted to me. "You'll come down low and then you can just let go."

"I c-c-can't. I'm too sc-scared!"

"Oh, Louisa!" Anna exclaimed anxiously. "What have you done?"

"She'll be hurt!" Elizabeth's frightened words reached me. "She'll fall and be killed!"

"No, she won't. Hang on, Susan," Willy called.

I kept my eyes shut tight. My fingers were clamped to the branch, and all I could think of was, I am going to die. I do not want to die. I want to be back on the ground.

Then there was a crackling of twigs very near me. I could hear Willy's uneven, quick breathing as he slowly edged his way nearer to me along the branch. From the distance came other, sharper sounds.

We are both going to die! I thought wildly, and I felt terrible for myself and even worse for my friend Willy, who also was doomed.

His weight along with mine bent the branch way down. I could feel it curving lower as the sharp, breaking sounds continued.

"Open your eyes and you'll see how close to the ground we are," he said. "You can jump off. You will be quite safe."

I squinched one eye open and saw the white fields swaying very close underneath. I forced my hands to let go, and I flew down, down, down, landing unhurt in a soft drift of snow.

A second later Willy dropped neatly from above, landing on his feet near me.

"Th-Thank you," I said. "You s-s-saved my life."

The others rushed over to us.

"I'm fine," I said. "I'm s-sorry I made such a fuss."

"Louisa shouldn't have . . . " Anna scolded, and Elizabeth nodded in agreement.

I felt called on to defend her. "It's the most exciting thing that ever happened to me in my whole life," I said. "I'd l-l-l—"

Anna puckered up her lips and blew, and I copied her. "I'd like to do it again."

"There," Louey said triumphantly. "She'd like to do it again. Taranta-ra!"

"Even so," Anna chided her, "it was very dangerous."

May came and slipped her little hand into mine. "You flew, Susan. You flew from the tree. Just like me and the birds." Her serious face made us all laugh.

I got to practice a dozen times, climbing up myself and then finally keeping my eyes wide open as I swung, before the bell called us in for a birthday celebration.

Sister Abigail had baked an apple cake with walnuts. Louey got presents from everyone: bookmarks and a fan and a lovely drawing and a pincushion and a heartfelt admiring poem from her father, who had spent the day writing and thinking.

With Aunt Nell guiding me, I had hemmed three cambric handkerchiefs, each with *LMA* stitched in green, and in the opposite corner I'd embroidered a really fine black-eyed Susan so that Louey would always remember me.

In the afternoon, Sister Abigail read *Rosamond* aloud to us while we girls sewed. Then Louey asked her mother to write a birthday message in her diary.

Sister Abigail wrote:

Your handwriting improves very fast. Take pains and do not be in a hurry. I like having you make observations about our conversations and your own thoughts. It helps you to express them and to understand your little self. Remember, dear girl, that a diary should be an epitome of your life. May it be a record of pure thoughts and good actions, then you will indeed be the precious child of your loving mother.

I thought that the loveliest present of all.

Afterward, Louey walked me through the snow to the rock fence. "It's been a wonderful birthday. I'll treasure the handkerchiefs forever. And never use them to wipe my nose!"

I went right home and told Aunt Nell all about the birthday celebration.

And after dinner, when she was resting her feet by the fireside, I told her about swinging from the tree. I'd thought of keeping it to myself, but that was sneaky, even though I'd never actually been forbidden to climb.

Flying

Aunt Nell probably never thought to forbid it because she knew my fear of heights. Why would she warn me about something that was the last thing in the world I'd ever want to do?

"Aunt Nell," I began. "I have something to tell you. I'm learning to climb trees and swing from branches."

She looked at me, alarm in her eyes. "Susan, what are you saying? You don't like high places. Even hills when we go walking, or steep roads."

"I tried climbing and swinging, and I like it. I'm real c-c-careful. It was hard at first, but I'm not scared anymore."

"It's not something girls do. Do the Alcott girls climb?"

"Mostly Louey. Her sisters can, but they don't enjoy it so much. I'm real good at it, Aunt. Why shouldn't I do it?"

She was quiet, thinking about it for a while. "No reason except custom, I guess," she said finally. "I climbed some when I was your age. I didn't tell my folks."

She sat with her hands idle in her lap for a bit. "Were you really very careful?"

I nodded. "I didn't go too high."

"And you did it with the other children? Never alone?"

Again, I nodded.

"You are very brave, child, and I'm proud of you." She put her arms around me and drew me close. "I'm glad you told me about it. Just be careful."

That was an easy promise to make. "Do you think I want to fall?"

She smoothed my hair.

"It's nice to be friends with someone, Aunt."

"You seem much happier since you've been going over there. I don't think it's done you anything but good. Even the climbing."

"I would like to be Louey's friend forever."

Aunt Nell sighed. "We like to hold on to the good things," she said. "But even after they are gone, we remember them with joy." There was sadness in her eyes.

She was talking about my ma, I realized, so I hugged her closer. Afterward, I understood she was talking about much more. She was talking about a person's whole life. And she was right. You've got to keep the good things in your head forever.

15. Giving Back

Next day, Willy came down with a cold that turned into a hacking cough. That, in turn, developed into a raging fever and sweats. Willy wasn't quiet and comfortable a single minute. It was the kind of sickness I knew well; I had had it often enough wintertimes. It just had to take its course.

First, Willy lay in his bed in his tiny upstairs room, face flushed, nose running, coughing day and night. Brother Charles sat beside him, nursing him and caring for him. He was a whole different person with his sick son. He was wonderfully sweet to Willy. He slept on a pallet on the sickroom floor.

"Let's move the invalid down into the common room," the schoolmaster suggested after several days of Willy's sickness. "It's much warmer down here. We'll leave the doors open and the kitchen fire will warm the rooms. And then we can all help care for him."

"I don't need help," Brother Charles said. "I can manage everything." Throughout Willy's illness he was determined to do all the caring for him. He turned from a being person into a doing person. I wouldn't have believed it was possible.

"But the warmth is important," the schoolmaster argued.

Finally, Willy was moved downstairs and the common room became the hospital.

The sickroom was closed to us. We drew pictures for him and sent in puzzles and stories. We sat in the kitchen and listened to whatever the grown-ups said, and we worried and hoped he'd get better soon. We children missed Willy. He had a sweetness about him that everyone liked.

For many days, Willy's fever did not break. During this time, Brother Charles was wonderful. Nobody ever had a better father, I own. He loved Willy very much and he'd do just about anything to help him.

What Willy liked most was to be read to, so his father read to him for hours and hours, patiently and kindly, first *Robinson Crusoe* then *Oliver Twist*.

Doing rather than being during Willy's sickness made Brother Charles's Inner Spirit grow. It didn't matter to him what he ate or drank or wore. I told that to Louey.

"Yes," she said, "someone should point his error out to him. But it better be a grown-up." Since her trouble with Sister Ann, Louey was careful not to correct adults.

Giving Back

The disease departed, leaving Willy weak and pale—but cheerful. Every single one of us was eager to do for Willy, to keep him company and read to him, to fetch things for him and to play with him. Aunt Nell gave me permission to sleep over at Fruitlands, so I could help Willy get well quickly.

And since no grown-ups pointed Brother Charles's error out to him, once Willy was better his father went back to his old, hard ways.

Without any warning, Brother Charles made a startling announcement at the lunch table. "Willy and I are off to join the Shakers once my boy is completely well. Eh, Willy?" He rubbed his hands enthusiastically.

Willy, pale with dark-shadowed eyes, looked up at his father. "Yes sir," he said.

Poor Willy, I thought. So weak and thin. You have to go. I'm positive you don't want to, but what can you do? If you speak out, there'll be a row, and it wouldn't do any good anyway.

"I am hoping that others here of like mind"—Brother Charles glanced at the schoolmaster and then at Brother Joseph—"will join with us as well."

Louey looked up at her mother in fear.

Sister Abigail shut her eyes for a moment but said nothing. She had said privately that she was weary of the nonsense talk about how being motherly was a selfish instinct. She was sick of hearing that a mother taking care of her own small family prevented a community of universal love. She was sick and tired of hearing about Shakers.

"No thank you. Not me." Brother Joseph declined the invitation right off. "Life in the Shaker village looks thin and regimented to me. I will go back to my family's farm."

The schoolmaster, looking very troubled, said, "I do not know what the best path is for my loved ones and me."

"Very well. I must go off to Boston briefly on business. When I return, Willy and I will leave. If you decide against the Shakers, you may stay on here till you have another place." Brother Charles paused, then added uncomfortably, "Stay, but you must not cut down any more wood or grind any more grain."

"How cruel," Sister Abigail exclaimed, "to leave children in the cold without firewood or bread!"

"I am truly sorry. But I put all my money into this venture. I must sell the place and try to get back what I can," Brother Charles reasoned.

"We have all given so much," she said sadly, looking around at the shambles of their dream.

Brother Charles packed up quickly, as if he couldn't afford to waste a second before he could be with the Shakers.

That very evening Sister Abigail asked me if I would sit with Willy till he fell asleep. "We Alcotts need to have a family meeting," she said. "Do you mind, Susan?"

Of course I didn't mind.

Louey, looking very frightened, spoke to me when we were alone. "Once Willy is asleep, you must slip quietly into the pantry and eavesdrop. I will leave the door ajar."

"I couldn't do that, Louey—"

"You must! Marmee thinks Father will break up our family and go with the Shakers! I'm so frightened, Susan. I don't know what to do. You're my best friend. I need you to be there."

"But what if I'm caught?'

"I'll tell that I put you up to it. Marmee will know you didn't do it on your own."

Willy was so tired from trying to walk around after weeks of being ill in bed, he fell asleep waiting for me to make my move in our chess game. Too bad. I might have won.

When I was sure he was sleeping soundly, I gathered up the chessmen and put them away. Then I took off my shoes and tiptoed into the cool pantry, leaving the door cracked open. I stood right behind the door, and I could hear Anna, Louey, and their parents, who were huddled near the grate. The younger girls were asleep upstairs.

"So now we must leave this place," Marmee was saying. "It is for you to decide how, Bronson."

"Our failure here is a terrible defeat. A great disappointment. It is so difficult, Abba. All my hopes and dreams..."

"I know, dear. Nevertheless, you must choose. We are your family, and I know we are very dear to you. Either we will all be together, or—" Her calm voice broke here.

I could hear soft sobbing. Louey.

Marmee spoke again in a firm, quiet voice. "I will not join the Shakers. I will keep my family as I know and love it. My brother Sam has written me that he will take rooms for me and the girls if I like. I have answered no. I will not break up my family. Now it is up to you."

"Let me think, dear," he begged. "Please let me think." Next minute, I heard his footsteps going up the stairs.

Hurriedly, I tiptoed back to Willy's bedside and put on my shoes.

"Thank you, Susan." Sister Abigail said when she came to relieve me. "Louey will tell you about our trouble."

"I—I know some," I said, stumbling. "I'm so sorry."

Sighing deeply, her mind elsewhere, she patted me on the shoulder. "That's all right," she said. "I know you love us."

Thus began a terrible night. In the attic where we slept, Anna and Louey wept softly. "I pray God to keep us all together," Louey whispered.

I, too, prayed for them.

Next morning, the schoolmaster did not come down from his bedroom. Nor did he appear afternoon or evening. Louey whispered to me that he had stopped eating and she feared he wanted to die. Her mother carried food and drink upstairs each mealtime, and then brought it back later untouched.

Two more days passed this way. Sister Abigail was weary. Anna tried a turn taking the tray up. Then Louey did it, and finally Elizabeth. He would not speak or even turn his head from the wall.

Secretly, I wished that I might have a turn.

Finally, on the fourth day, when the lunch tray of fresh toast and apples and water was ready and Sister Abigail looked around, I grew bold. "May I take up the schoolmaster's lunch?" I asked.

"Why, of course you may, Susan. It would make him happy to see you," she said, handing me the tray.

Up I went very very carefully. Hesitantly, I knocked at the door. "Brother Bronson? It is Susan with your tray. May I come in?"

There was a muffled answer which I took to be yes. I wasn't sure, but I wanted it to be yes, so I opened the door.

The room was dark and cold, and Brother Bronson was huddled on the bed.

I set the tray on the small bedside cabinet and just stood there in the dismal darkness. I turned to go.

But then I turned back again, and I spoke to the shape on the bed. "Schoolmaster, I have come to say thank you for what you and Fruitlands have done for me."

He stirred but did not turn.

"I could not talk before you came here. I did not really know how to think. I had no friends and my life was sad. My pa was 'shamed of me. But since Fruitlands I am reborn." My voice faltered, for by then I was crying.

"Do not weep, child," he said hoarsely, and turned his head toward me.

"I just wanted to tell you that for me, Fruitlands was not a failure. It has given me back my life."

Here I stopped, for I had nothing further to say.

"Thank you, Susan," he said softly.

I waited, hoping for more words. And, at last, more came. Blessed words.

"I will have some toast, after all. I am famished. Please ask Sister Abigail to come up."

I ran out of there so fast, I barked my shins on a trunk. For speed I slid down the banister. "He's eating the toast!" I called down as I slid. "He wants to see you, Sister Abigail!"

She hastened up the stairs, and we waited soundlessly

below, looking up. Finally she emerged and started down, smiling, carrying the empty tray. "He's had the toast and the apple," she told us. "His faith has given him strength. He's coming down. All will be well."

Then she kissed me on top of my head. "Bless you, Susan," was all she said. It was enough. I knew that I had given a few words back in exchange for the many words that had been given me.

When Brother Charles returned, he packed quickly so that he could depart for his new utopia. Willy waited till the very last minute to say good-bye to me. "Practice chess, Susan," he said. "You will be a wizard of a player." He put out his hand.

"Good-bye, Willy. I'll miss you." I shook his hand. "You are almost like a brother to me."

"You couldn't have a brother who speaks English so strangely." There was a twinkle in his eyes now. He was ragging me.

"Maybe the Shakers will teach you to speak like a Yankee."

My mention of the Shakers drove away the twinkle. Then he managed a weak grin.

"I'm jolly glad to be your friend, Susan."

"Me too."

* * *

"Now we must leave as quickly as possible," Sister Abigail said.

"But we have no money," her husband said with despair. "And no place to go."

"Not true," she said. "I have already made inquiries. Mr. Lovejoy in Still River—which is not too far for us to manage to travel to—will rent us three rooms and the use of the kitchen for fifty cents a week.

"I have sold my cloak for twelve dollars and a silver plate that was a wedding present for another ten. Further, my brother Sam has sent ten more. And Mr. Emerson has offered to help if we are in need.

"We will take the rooms for the winter. You can cut wood and do carpentry and in the spring we will move on. You can be a schoolmaster again."

"Abba, you are my hope and my strength," he said. "When Susan came upstairs, I was in the depths of despair. Her words brought light and reminded me how kind and good and loving you and my girls are. It was those thoughts—of the goodness of my family and how blessed I really am—that brought me forth to live. And we shall live and be happy and hope once again!"

A week later, on the day they were to leave, Pa and I walked over for the last time. On Pa's shoulder was a hamper of bread and jam and fruit that Aunt Nell had packed for their travel lunch. In my hands I carried a fresh cheese, which Aunt Nell had insisted I take.

"But they don't eat cheese, Aunt Nell," I'd argued.

"They *didn't* eat cheese. But that first day, Louisa said the girls all loved cheese—till that Brother Charles came along and condemned it. Now he's gone and good riddance. Carry the cheese, child."

I obeyed.

Sister Abigail received the hamper from Pa gratefully. Then I handed her my bundle wrapped in a damp white cloth.

"What's this, a cheese?" She smiled. "Bless your aunt Nell. Bronson!" she called up the stairs. "Miss Wilson has sent the children a cheese. Is that not kind of her? You remember how much they love cheese."

He came out onto the landing, hammer in hand. "Yes," he said. "I remember." He paused to consider. "Such a loving gift can do them no harm," he decided. "We have been blessed with kind neighbors."

He set the hammer on the top stair and came down to meet us.

"I have been thinking, Neighbor Wilson, that perhaps once we are settled your Susan could come and stay with us. That way I could go on teaching her and helping her speak easily."

Pa drew back a step. "I don't know," he said, frowning. "Her aunt Nell would miss her something fierce." He stopped and looked down at me. He was really looking at me, looking into my eyes, not like in the old days when he looked past me and didn't really see me at all.

He finished up his talking. "And me too. I'd miss her myself. She's the breath of life on our farm."

His words sent lightness into my heart such as I'd not felt before. I didn't know if they'd ask my opinion, and I didn't wait to be asked. "Thank you, but I want to stay at home with my folks," I said. And I curtseyed just 'cause I felt like it.

"Your daughter is a clever and sensitive child," the schoolmaster went on. "It has been a privilege to teach her. Let her read and learn so that she may, one day, teach others. There is no higher calling."

Pa nodded.

The schoolmaster then handed me a thick book bound in black cloth with scarlet edging. "The little paper diary we gave you will soon be full, Susan. Once it is, you may move on to write your thoughts in this book."

I clasped his hand. "Thank you, sir, for everything."

"Look what I have," Louey interrupted, picking up a large envelope from which she carefully drew a freshly hand-printed copy of *Susan and the Copperhead*. On its white pasteboard cover was a fierce snake drawn in crayon by Elizabeth. There it was, the coppery head atop the hazel-colored body with hourglass markings on top and a pinkish white belly with dark markings below.

Turning the pages, I found that every other page was an illustration: First there was the snake lying in wait of us; then May and me walking toward the spring; me holding May while she drank; me drinking; me seeing the reflection of May holding the snake; finally, me grabbing the snake and flinging it away.

"It's a real book," I said.

"It's for you to keep," she said proudly. "*Susan and the Copperhead* is my first book, and since you are the heroine and it is really your story, you must have it. Promise to keep it always and remember me."

"I promise, Louey," I said.

"Always?"

"Always and a day more."

"That's just about long enough to be best friends," she said.

Dear Diary,

They are gone.

Fruitlands is empty, though the sign still swings in front of the old red farmhouse. My friends have moved off to Still River. Though I am sorry not to have them nearby, I am glad they are in a warm, safe place.

Louey will write letters to me when she can, and Aunt Nell says I may always have postage to answer her. I'd love to get letters from her. She wrote the best play ever. I am proud to be her friend.

I'm still a little pitcher with giant ears. Yesterday, Brother Joseph came by to tell Pa he bought the farm from Brother Charles and will bring his wife to live there. "We will farm," he said, "but we will also keep it as an open house for Come-Outers and wayfarers."

"How's that?" Pa asked.

"A pot of stew, a seat by the fireside, and a book will always be ready for the weary traveler," Brother Joseph said. "And Susan must come and use the library as if it's her own."

"I welcome you as a neighbor." Pa offered his hand for a hearty shake.

"Beard and all?" Brother Joseph asked.

"Yes, beard and all," Pa said. "I welcome you."

"Then the Fruitlands experiment has been a success."

"How do you reckon that?" Pa asked.

"Well, it's taught you to like me, and I've learned to admire and like you, and the two of us will live side by side in peace."

"And how about me?" I boldly joined the adults' conversation. "I have learned to speak without stammering. And I learned about Socrates and Penelope and Cleopatra and how to read better—"

"Whoa there!" Pa chuckled. "Fruitlands has turned my silent girl into a chess-playing chatterbox."

Giving Back

Aunt Nell, who'd been listening to all of this talk, put in her two cents' worth now. "Yes, " she said, smoothing my hair, "and that's the miracle of it. We should ever be grateful."

"Amen!" Brother Joseph said, looking toward Fruit-lands, and Pa echoed it.

And in my heart, it resounded loudest of all.

Author's Note

In 1843, when Louisa May Alcott was ten, her father, along with some like-minded friends, bought a farm. Intent on building a paradise on earth, they came to live together at Fruitlands as one family. They shared work, food, and ideas, and disdained money. They were striving to be the very best that humans could be: spiritually pure and honorable and good. They called themselves Consociates, and the philosophy that guided them was called Transcendentalism.

Little Women Next Door tells the story of how Louisa May Alcott and these well-meaning adult-dreamers, who would not drink milk because it robbed the cow or wear wool because it robbed the sheep, affected the life of Susan, a lonely, rather ordinary girl on the next farm.

Susan Wilson and her family are completely my invention; therefore, the friendship between Susan and Louisa and the other children is fiction, as, of course, is the dialogue. All of the other characters are based on real people and the major events actually occurred at Fruitlands.

Bronson Alcott was an educator; his co-founder of Fruitlands, Charles Lane, was a British philosopher. The other Consociates varied in background; all were opposed to slavery.

The Consociates were journal-keepers and writers, so Bronson Alcott and Charles Lane wrote and published much about their Paradise. What the Consociates thought, wore, and ate, and what their daily life was like, they amply documented. In addition, there are hundreds of other valuable sources. Madeleine B. Stern's biography, *Louisa May Alcott,* is a delightful and comprehensive study of Louisa's life. *Marmee: The Mother of Little Women* by Sandford Salyer is intriguing and very informative, as is *Lost Utopias* by Harriet E. O'Brien. Most important and entertaining is Louisa May Alcott's own *Transcendental Wild Oats—And Excerpts From the Fruitlands Diaries,* written thirty years after the Fruitlands experiment.

Because the Alcotts were remarkable, if eccentric, reading about them for *Little Women Next Door* was always interesting. But the best part of my research took me to the Concord area and the two Alcott dwellings, which are now both fine museums.

First is the Fruitlands Museum, with a rare library (in the old farm-house near Harvard Village). Fruitlands afforded me the opportunity to explore the home and grounds. It also includes a wealth of information on nineteenth-century American history: a Shaker museum, an Indian museum, and a picture gallery. Second, Orchard House in Concord, the Alcotts' permanent family home, is filled with treasures: furniture and per-sonal possessions and manuscripts.

Not too far away is peaceful Sleepy Hollow Cemetery, where the Alcotts rest under plain, modest gravestones alongside some great American writers: Henry Thoreau, Ralph Waldo Emerson, and Nathaniel Hawthorne.

While my book ends with the closing of Fruitlands, the lives of the real people in it continued. Bronson Alcott became superintendent of the Concord public schools. He reformed them and had a long and distin-guished career as a teacher, writer, and philosopher. However, he never earned much money.

Charles Lane left the Shakers to return to England, where he remarried and had five more children. (So much for his prejudice against families.)

And Louisa grew up to be a very great writer and supported her fam-ily all her life through her writing.